# 'TWAS THE NIGHT BEFORE SCANDAL

MERRY FARMER

**'TWAS THE NIGHT BEFORE SCANDAL**

Copyright ©2020 by Merry Farmer

Cover design by Erin Dameron-Hill (the miracle-worker)

ASIN: B08HDDMSRZ

Paperback ISBN: 9798683788988

Click here for a complete list of other works by Merry Farmer.

If you'd like to be the first to learn about when the next books in the series come out and more, please sign up for my newsletter here: http://eepurl.com/RQ-KX

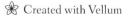 Created with Vellum

CHAPTER 1

LONDON – JUST BEFORE CHRISTMAS, 1887

*C*hristmas was only a few days away, and Lady
Beatrice Lichfield still didn't have an engagement ring on her finger. That fact wouldn't have caused
her distress as she worked, tying bows with sprigs of holly
for the decorations that were going up all over the rented
hall in Clerkenwell, where the May Flowers were
holding their charity event for the benefit of several
London orphanages. In fact, not wearing jewelry of any
sort was a great boon when it came to the delicate work
she was required to do with her hands to create the decorations. And no shiny bobbles meant that some of the
more mischievous orphans who were helping with preparations weren't tempted.

But it had been months—no, years—since Bea had set

her heart on Lord Harrison Manfred, Marquess of Landsbury. They'd been a part of the same group of friends ever since Bea joined the May Flowers and made the acquaintance of the likes of Lady Diana Pickwick, her very best friend in the entire world, Cecelia Campbell—who was now Lady Marlowe—and Bianca Marlowe —who was now Lady Clerkenwell and the hostess of the event. Through her female connections, Bea had been introduced to Harrison, and as far as she was concerned, it was love at first sight.

She'd always thought Harrison felt the same way, but as she stood at the long table, piled high with loose ribbon, boughs of holly and pine, wire to craft the decorations with, and bits and pieces of donations that had been delivered to the hall, staring at her sadly naked fingers, she heaved a sigh.

"What sort of silly, maudlin thoughts are going through your head to cause such a sigh?" Diana asked with a sardonic grin, stripping excess leaves off a sprig of holly for her decorations.

Bea glanced guiltily up at her friend, knowing full well what Diana thought of the situation. Diana was as brilliant and prickly as the holly she worked with—lovely and useful, but full of unexpected spikes and barbs. She was a beauty of the highest order as well, with dark hair and eyes, a clear, pale complexion, and a figure that made London's finest modistes compete for her custom. By contrast, Bea considered herself sallow and skinny, with too much strawberry-blonde hair and eyes that couldn't decide whether they were blue or green. No wonder Harrison was taking his time deciding whether he wanted to be shackled to her for the remainder of his life.

"I'm merely anxious that we won't be able to finish decorating in time for the party on Christmas Eve," she said, though she was a terrible liar. Her cheeks flared bright pink every time she so much as thought something dishonest.

Diana's grin was all the proof she needed that her friend could see right through her. "Christmas Eve is still three days away, dearest. Which gives us ample time not only to finish decorating this hall, as shabby and cavernous as it is—" She glanced up at the rafters and around at the vast, bustling room in all its run-down glory. "—but to collect enough clothing, toys, and essentials to give half the orphans in East London the very merriest of Christmases."

"You're right." Bea forced herself to smile and take a breath to clear her head. "I suppose I'm overly worried for nothing."

Her attention was drawn to the door at the far side of the room as soon as she was finished speaking. Harrison had just entered, along with his close friend, Lord John Darrow, Viscount Whitlock—who also happened to be Diana's arch-nemesis—carrying a tall pine tree between them. Bea's heart ran riot in her chest, thumping against her ribs and causing her to gulp for breath. Harrison was simply the handsomest man she'd ever laid eyes on. He was tall and well-formed, like so many of the cricket players he and John idolized. His face was kindness personified, with soulful, hazel eyes that displayed his emotions as though they were a stage. He smiled at several of the orphans who were there to help with decorations as they rushed to see the tree, saying something to them that Bea couldn't hear from the other side of the room, but that she was certain was full of sweetness and wisdom.

She'd longed to be Harrison's wife from the moment he'd asked her to waltz with him at the ball where they'd met. His arms had felt so sure and certain around her, and the way he'd smiled at her and asked gentle, interesting questions to get to know her as they danced made her feel as though she were the most important woman in the—

"If you were any more obvious, the fire brigade would barge through the doors to douse you with ice water, Bea," Diana snapped at Bea's side.

"What? Oh, I—" Bea's face flared even hotter. She snapped her head down to focus on the bow she was tying, only to discover that she'd made three knots and trapped her fingers between the ribbon. "I was just...." She gave up her attempt at an explanation with a sigh. Diana knew the truth of things anyhow.

"I don't see how you could care for a man who spends so much of his time in the company of an absolute bounder," Diana growled, staring daggers across the room at Lord John. Although, if Bea's guess was right, the heat in Diana's eyes every time she glared at John was of a different sort than what Diana imagined it to be. "I see it as a distinct lack of character that your beau has such wicked friends."

"Lord John isn't wicked." Bea broke into a grin and sent Diana a sideways look. "And Harrison is simply wonderful for volunteering his time for the May Flowers's cause. He's a gentleman and a peer, and there are a great many other things he could be doing at Christmastime instead of decorating a public hall in Clerkenwell for the sake of orphans."

"Yes, well, I'm certain that Bianca turned the thumbscrews on that entire lot, forcing them to help with preparations when they would much rather have been lazing about their club, smoking cigars and gambling."

Bea laughed out loud at the image. "Harrison doesn't care for smoking," she said, her laugh turning into a sigh as she watched him and John anchor their tree in a stand and secure it. "He does care for charitable causes. Why, just the other day, at Lady Hartnell's Christmas concert, he was telling me how passionate he is about supporting the downtrodden and funding those men and women who work on their behalf."

Diana hummed suspiciously, her gaze set on John. "I would wager he said that in order to impress you. Most likely so that you would slip into the next room with him and let him take liberties." A spark of longing lit her eyes as she spoke, still studying John.

"Harrison would never be so inconsiderate," Bea said with a knowing grin. That grin faded quickly, though.

Harrison hadn't once taken liberties with her. The most passionate thing he'd done in the years that they'd known and flirted with each other was to remove her glove so that he could kiss her bare hand. And while that had taken her breath away, she would be lying to herself if she said she hadn't wanted more.

"Why hasn't he proposed yet?" she whispered passionately.

Her accidental outburst happened just as Bianca crossed behind her and Diana. Bianca stopped and rocked back to stand between Bea and Diana, staring across the room at Harrison and John as they finished with the tree, then rushed to help a man who had just brought several boxes of donations through the door.

"Are you still waiting for Harrison to propose?" Bianca asked, the side of her mouth twitching into a grin.

Bea pulled her gaze away from Harrison to stare guiltily at Bianca. "I'm afraid that at this point, it's not going to happen."

"Nonsense," Bianca snorted. "That man has been besotted with you for at least two years."

"Perhaps." Bea lowered her eyes, wanting to believe it but not letting herself hope.

Bianca stared at her like she had spit on her mother's grave. "You can't possibly tell me that you think the man would do anything *but* propose," she said.

"It hasn't happened yet, so I despair of it happening at all," Bea said.

Bianca shook her head. "And here I thought you were intelligent."

"Bea is intelligent," Diana said, back to glaring across the room as Harrison and John took the new boxes of donations to a table that was already overloaded with various crates, sacks, and parcels of clothing, toys, and necessities. "It's men who lack basic intelligence."

Again, Bianca laughed. "You're not wrong," she said, then laid a hand on Bea's shoulder. "He'll propose, ducky. I know it. A man doesn't look at a woman the way Harrison looks at you without marriage on his mind. And besides, it's nearly Christmas. What better time to ask a woman to spend the whole rest of her life with him than at Christmas?"

"If you say so," Bea said with a wistful sigh.

She tried to return to tying bows, but her heart, her thoughts, and her eyes flew back to Harrison at the other end of the room. She would have given anything to know if he planned to marry her or if she'd been imagining his regard for her. She only wished she would work up the nerve to let him know that, if he asked for her hand, her answer would be a resounding yes.

"I'M MERELY SAYING THAT THE MOMENT HAS TO BE perfect," Harrison said to John as he wedged the box filled with musty-smelling clothes and old shoes onto the table that was already overflowing with donations. "A

7

man only gets once chance to propose to the woman of his dreams, and I'm determined to get it right."

John laughed at him, of course, slapping him on the back as soon as he'd found a place on the crowded table for the load of old coats in his arms. "You're the most maudlin man I know," he said. "I swear, you should have been born a poet, not a peer."

"No man is born a poet," Harrison said with a grin, pushing a few boxes around on the table to make room for more. "Poetry is inspired in a man by the beauty and perfection of his subject."

He pivoted to glance across the room at Lady Beatrice. Bea really was the most extraordinary woman he'd ever met. She was kind and gentle while still being strong and passionate about the causes the May Flowers stood for. Where Lady Diana and some of the others waved their fists and bullied the audiences they spoke to about women's rights and Ireland, Beatrice spoke reason in a quiet voice, convincing even the most stubborn old men that she might have a point. And she was gorgeous, though he suspected she didn't know it. Her hair was the most enticing reddish-blonde color, her lips were rosy and full, and her eyes were a unique shade of blue-green that he'd found himself lost in on more than one occasion. He couldn't count the number of nights he'd lain awake, tossing and turning with desire for her to the point where he'd had to take care of things on his own just to put himself out of his misery. And yet, with all the pent-up desire he had for Bea, he would never in a million years have importuned her honor by putting her in a position she might not have been comfortable with.

"You're a besotted fool," John laughed, shaking his head. "Why torture yourself waiting for the perfect moment to come along? It's not the proposal, or the wedding, that matters, it's the life you two were meant to have together. Get on with it."

"I intend to," Harrison said, excitement shooting through him.

He glanced around to make sure as few people as possible were close enough to listen in, going so far as to nudge John's arm and gesture for him to walk to the end of the table where fewer people were milling about. Once they were separated and in relative privacy, Harrison reached into the inner pocket of his jacket and took out a small, old, velvet box. With a proud look and a flutter in his overly-sentimental heart, he opened the box to show John the ring inside.

"Why, Harrison," John said, his mouth twitching into a grin as his eyes danced with teasing. "I had no idea you felt this way. Yes, yes, I'll marry you."

"No, you dolt." Harrison let out an impatient breath, knowing full well his friend was ribbing him. "It's a family ring," he went on in a whisper. "I had a formal audience with my grandmother just the other day to inform her of my intentions to ask for Lady Beatrice's hand. Grandmama presented me with this ring, which belonged to her mother, one Lady Caroline Herrington."

"Well, there you have it," John said with a shrug. "So

9

get over there, go down on one knee, and propose." He nodded across the room to where Bea and Diana had taken a handful of red bows to fasten to a pine garland that was draped over a tall, wide fireplace.

"Not here," Harrison said, closing the lid of the box. "And not now."

"Then when and where?" John asked, crossing his arms.

"Christmas Eve," Harrison said. "After the party for the orphans is finished. I'll offer to take Bea home, but I plan to whisk her off to a particularly beautiful spot overlooking the Thames. I'll propose there."

John shook his head. "You're making things overly complicated. You don't need family rings and picturesque backdrops. Bea would marry you if you'd tripped in a mud puddle, splashed her favorite gown in the process, and asked the question while still wallowing in the grime."

"But why be cavalier about something so important when you can make an impression?" Harrison asked. "Or are you just cynical because Diana would laugh in your face if you proposed to her?"

John's brow shot up with mock offense. "I would have you know that if I proposed to Diana right now, she would—"

He didn't get a chance to finish his boast. A crash sounded from the other end of the room, along with a yelp that Harrison knew in an instant belonged to Bea. He rushed forward, depositing the ring box on the edge of the table as he went, and rushed to Bea's aid, John right behind him.

"Bea, are you all right?" he asked, heart pounding with worry, as he and John reached the fireplace. A small stepstool lay on its side, and the pine garland Bea was attaching bows to was half torn off, the end trailing on the floor, too close to the fire for comfort.

"I'm fine," Bea said, the most gorgeous blush on her porcelain face as she straightened and brushed pine needles from her skirt. "I simply lost my balance on the stool is all. It's silly really."

"Here, let me help you." Harrison bent to set the stool upright. Bea watched him, her eyes lowered fetchingly, her shapely mouth stretching into a smile as she did. "Now, just allow me to fasten this bough to the mantle again and you'll be able to hang your bows."

"Thank you, Harrison." The tenderness in Bea's eyes was all the gift Harrison needed that Christmas.

"Lady Diana, I would have expected you to take better care of your friend," John told Diana in a mock scolding voice.

"Oh, you would, would you?" Diana crossed her arms and glared at John. "And I suppose you would have done a better job of hanging bows?"

"I do a better job of just about everything than you do, pet," John said, deliberately antagonizing her.

Diana let out an outraged huff and stomped her foot before marching back to the table where supplies for making bows were scattered.

Harrison exchanged a knowing look with Bea as she stepped onto the stool to hand her bows. The moment of connection was priceless.

"They'll be the death of each other someday," he said, adding a wink.

"I'm certain they will be," Bea replied in an intimate voice.

Maybe John was right and he was a sap after all, but Harrison couldn't help but be thrilled at the brief exchange. It was as though the rest of the world had disappeared, leaving just the two of them and the need that pulsed between them. He could have stayed by Bea's side all day, helping her with whatever task she needed help with, being her devoted servant. He assisted her with hanging bows for as long as he could, but all too soon, she needed to return to her table to craft a few more.

"Thank you again for your help," she said as Harrison moved around the table and worked up his will to leave her side.

"Anything you need from me," he said, hovering on the other side of the table from her for a moment. At last, he let out a sigh and turned to head back across the room to the other set of tables. He'd collect his great-grand-mother's ring, pry John away from Lady Diana long enough to head out for a spot of coffee, and figure out exactly how to orchestrate the perfect proposal, and then—

He stopped dead, his heart sinking into his stomach

as he glanced across the room only to find the table where he'd put the ring completely empty. Dread filled him as he strode across the room, careful not to arouse Bea's suspicions—he still wanted the proposal to come as a surprise, after all, and if she had reason to ask why he was running across the room all of a sudden, he'd have to explain the ring—hoping that his eyes deceived him.

But no, the donations table was completely empty, not a scrap of anything that had once been there in sight.

# CHAPTER 2

*P*anic hit Harrison like a cannonball in the gut. He picked up his pace, reaching the empty table at the far end of the room and staring at it as though everything that had been there just moments before would return. He walked around the table, bent to search underneath, and twisted this way and that, perplexed about where everything had gone and how it had disappeared so fast.

"Something wrong, my lord?" one of the women who was volunteering along with the May Flowers asked as she carried a wide basket filled with toys to another table.

"Um, er, no. That is to say...nothing's wrong," Harrison stammered.

He didn't know why he was so reticent about telling the woman he'd put a ring on the table and lost it. She seemed to be a good enough sort, although from what he understood, several of the younger, rougher women helping out with preparations for the party were actually whores. Bianca had a habit of befriending all sorts, whether they were bent on reformation or not, and it wouldn't have surprised Harrison if some of the women in the room had customers waiting for them once they were finished volunteering. He didn't want to give anyone, least of all Bea, even a fleeting suspicion that he would ever entertain the notion of paying that sort of woman a visit

The woman in question furrowed her brow at him for a moment, as though she thought he were barmy, before walking on. He probably was barmy. Only a first-rate fool would abandon a priceless family heirloom on a table in the middle of a crowded room.

He turned back to the table once the woman had moved on, running his hands over the table's surface as if by some miracle the ring had fallen into a crack or sunk into a portal to another world. The idea was ridiculous, but far less painful than the notion that he'd lost it.

"What on earth are you doing, man?" John asked, striding up to Harrison with a bemused look on his face.

"Did you see what happened to the things that were on this table?" Harrison whispered, glancing around as though everyone would overhear and know how big of a fool he was.

"No." John shrugged. "What happened to them?" he asked, as though Harrison had asked some sort of riddle.

"I don't know," Harrison hissed. "I was hoping you saw where they went."

John flushed slightly. "I'm afraid I was too engaged with the lovely and irascible Lady Diana to notice much of anything, let alone what happened to a pile of old rubbish."

"It wasn't rubbish, it was donations for the local orphanages," Harrison said, continuing to look around. He edged his way to the next table, picking through its contents to see if the ring box had been moved there. But all that table contained was more of the same clothing, toys, and sundries that people were bringing in.

"I know you're of a charitable mindset," John said, grinning as he followed Harrison from table to table, "but this concern is a bit daft, don't you think?"

Harrison stopped his frantic search and turned to his friend. "My great-grandmother's ring was on that table."

John lost his smug look, his eyes suddenly going wide. "You put the ring on the table?" When Harrison nodded sheepishly, John laughed and shook his head. "Why didn't you put it back in your jacket where it came from?"

"Bea needed me," Harrison explained, his face heating even more. "I didn't think about where I was putting the ring. I didn't think about anything but rushing to help her."

"Of course, you didn't," John said with a smirk. "I think the entire building could be burning and you wouldn't think about anything but shielding Bea's pretty little head from all the ash raining down."

"You're right, of course," Harrison said, continuing his search of the tables nearest the one that had been cleared. "Even though I know you're being an arse. But there isn't time for that. Help me find what happened to the ring."

John heaved a long-suffering sigh and set to work, moving through the tables with Harrison and scanning their contents. Everything looked the same—so much so that for a few, fleeting moments of hope, Harrison thought that he hadn't set the ring on the table that had been cleared after all, but had set it on another table. A few more minutes of searching and picking through things proved that to be a false hope, though.

"It's gone," Harrison said at last, once he and John had circled back to the empty table. "Grandmama is going to murder me. And as for Bea—"

He glanced wistfully to the other side of the room, where Bea was deep in conversation with Diana as the two of them constructed more bows. Bea glanced up and met his gaze, her cheeks flushing in a way that was so beautiful it made Harrison's trousers tight. But there was no time for any of that.

He jerked his head back to John. "What am I going to do?" he hissed, panic on the verge of getting the best of him.

John looked around as though an answer would spring up out of nowhere. A few seconds later, a young lad in worn but clean clothes and a cap strode up to the empty table with a new box of donations.

"Excuse me," John addressed him. "Do you know what happened to the things that were on this table?"

"Yes, I do, my lord," the lad answered with a cheeky grin.

Harrison was so overwhelmed with relief that he didn't care that the lad was being clever with him. "Where has it all gone?" he asked.

"That depends," the lad answered, then waited for the banter to continue.

"Depends on what?" John asked, narrowing his eyes as if to tell the boy they wouldn't stand for his cheek.

"On who carried what out," the boy said.

Harrison let out a breath, rubbing a hand over his face. "Son, we really don't have time for this."

"Although we might have time to string you up by your ankles," John growled.

The lad saw that the time for joking was over. "All the stuff from this table was taken out to three carts, and each of those was heading to a different orphanage."

Harrison gaped at him. "Three different orphanages?"

"Yessir, my lord. One to Hope Orphanage in Hackney, and the other two to Mr. Siddel's orphanage and to the Sisters of Perpetual Sorrow in Limehouse."

Harrison and John exchanged a look. "Are you familiar with either of those places?" Harrison asked.

"No." John shrugged and shook his head. "Are you?"

"No." Harrison let out a breath of disappointment, deeply worried that his family ring was gone.

"I know where they all are," the lad said.

Harrison and John both turned to him.

"What's your name, lad?" John asked.

"Burt, my lord," Burt said with a wide smile. "And for tuppence, I can take you to them all."

The hope Harrison thought he'd lost returned. He reached into his pocket and took out a small coin. "There you go, Burt. And there will be more where that came from if we find a certain item I've lost."

"What item is that, my lord?" Burt asked, a gleam in his eyes.

"Never you mind, scamp," John answered, turning Burt by his shoulders toward the door. "Lead the way. We've got to recover Lord Linfield's lost heart so he can propose to his sweetheart."

"Oh, so it's about love, is it?" Burt asked, hurrying ahead, Harrison and John behind him.

"It is," Harrison admitted. And if he didn't find the ring so that he could surprise Bea with the most perfect proposal ever, he didn't know what he would do with himself.

Bea watched Harrison and John flitter around the far end of the room as Diana prattled on about how much better the world would be if women were in charge. She was utterly puzzled about what Harrison could possibly be doing, darting back and forth as he was. He didn't seem to have any aim other than studying the items that had been donated. She couldn't think what possible interest any of the donations could have for him, but there didn't seem to be any other explanation for his searching.

And then he left. Just like that. Without saying goodbye to her. He and John rushed out, following a young lad called Burt that had been running errands for Bianca and some of the others all morning. As soon as Harrison left the room, Bea felt as though her heart fled with him.

"...and with all the new organizations forming around the issue of women's suffrage, I think it's only a matter of time before we see not only women gaining the vote, we'll see them elected to Parliament as well. And once that happens—Heavens, Bea, are you paying any attention at all?" Diana asked with a huff, throwing the ribbon she'd just finished tying down on the table.

"What? Oh. Hmm?" Flustered and blushing, Bea dragged her eyes away from the doorway Harrison had disappeared out of and focused her gaze on Diana.

Diana tilted her head to one side and pursed her lips as she studied Bea. "The sun does not rise and set dependent on whether Harrison Manfred is in the room."

"I know, I know," Bea sighed, letting her shoulders drop as she tried to concentrate on her work. "It's just that...I wish...if he would only...."

"Get on with it and propose marriage," Diana finished, rolling her eyes. "Believe me. You make it hard for me to think of anything else."

"I'm sorry." Bea set aside her newly finished bow and gathered up materials to make another one. "I'm a bore, I know. It's just that I love him so, and it makes me so anxious every time he runs out on me like this."

"Well, wherever he was running off to," Diana said, tilting her nose up and staring at the doorway, "he can't be up to any good. Not if he's with John."

Bea nearly laughed in spite of herself. She and Diana made quite a pair. Both of them pined after the men they loved like silly schoolgirls, but they each had different ways of doing it. But Bea wasn't sure whether it was more effective to long wistfully for a man or to pretend that she couldn't stand him.

She had only begun to contemplate the question when the two middle-class ladies, Bianca's neighbors in Clerkenwell, who had just carried in fresh armfuls of greenery launched into a curious conversation.

"Treacle all over everything," the dark-haired one said, her eyes round. "It was a right mess to clean up."

"Over their schoolbooks and everything?" the grey-haired one asked.

"As if the books were toast," the dark-haired one answered with a nod. "The whole lot of them were ruined."

"Books don't come cheap," the grey-haired one agreed. "Whoever done it should be horsewhipped, if you ask me."

"What's this all about?" Bianca asked as she walked up to the table to sort the new greenery.

"If you please, Lady Clerkenwell," the grey-haired

lady said, bobbing a quick curtsy. "Someone's gone and pulled a prank at St. Joseph's Orphanage."

"They rigged a bucket of treacle to fall all over Sister Mary's desk," the dark-haired woman said.

"Good Lord." Bianca's eyes went wide. "That sounds like the sort of prank Rupert and I used to play on our German governess when we were children."

"That's exactly what it sounds like," Diana agreed, sending Bea a look as though pranks were played on governesses all the time.

Bea assumed she was right, though she and her sisters had never been so bold as to tease their governess in any way. Madame Julienne was the closest thing they had had to a mother, after their own mother died in child-birth. But the idea of pranks had always fascinated Bea.

"A whole pile of books was ruined, my lady," the dark-haired woman continued to tell the story to Bianca. "And books are precious, they are."

"I agree," Bianca said in her take-charge voice. "I'll be certain to pay a visit to St. Joseph's to assess their needs, and I'll purchase all new books for them as soon as our party and the Christmas holidays are over."

"Bless you, Lady Clerkenwell," the grey-haired lady said, beaming as though Bianca were an angel. "You sure have been a boon to this community."

As soon as the two ladies moved on, Bianca slid closer to Bea and Diana. "Can you imagine what the likes of Claudia Denbigh would say if they heard how much of an angel I am?" she laughed.

Bea laughed along with her, knowing full well that Bianca had made more enemies than friends among the ranks of the aristocracy because of her wild ways. Bea was secretly in awe of Bianca herself, particularly Bianca's amazing ability to get along with people of all classes and to treat everyone as though they were equals. Then again, Bianca had married a man who had been born in a brothel, even if he was a lord now. That had been entirely Lord Malcolm Campbell's doing. Lord Malcolm, as everyone knew him, whether it was the proper form of address or not, had married Bianca's mother just the year before, but he had been a friend of the Marlowe family for decades, and he was one of the most powerful men in England. Which made it even more astonishing that Bianca could move so freely in middle-class circles as well as higher ones.

"I saw the way you drooped like a blossom in the frost when Harrison dashed out of here," Bianca said, jolting Bea out of her thoughts.

"Oh," Bea said, using the excuse of reaching for wire to tie the bow she was making to lower her eyes. Bianca was likely to see the truth in her expression if she didn't. "It's nothing. I was just...." She couldn't think of a way to finish her sentence.

"Patience, ducky, that's all you need," Bianca said with a wink. "Just a little patience."

"Bea has no patience," Diana laughed. "She is consumed by love, and if it remains unrequired, she'll expire, like a maiden in some medieval tale."

They all shared a laugh, though Bea had to admit there was a certain degree of truth to the joking accusation. She was veering closer and closer to desperation with every day that passed.

Bianca seemed to notice. Her expression changed from teasing to contemplative, and she studied Bea with a calculating look.

"Mama and Lord Malcolm were dead-set against me marrying Jack," she said, as though speaking her thoughts aloud. "But I won that battle in the end. And do you know how I did it?"

"I can't imagine," Bea said, her face flaring hot, unable to meet Bianca's eyes. In fact, Bea—and everyone else in society—knew exactly how Bianca had won the right to marry Jack Craig. He'd gotten her with child, and Bianca had been too stubborn for a lightning-fast marriage to a more suitable groom to cover the fact.

"Determination," Bianca answered, a light in her eyes that said she knew full well what Bea had been thinking. "You may think it was the other thing," she went on, looking extraordinarily proud of herself when most people would have said she should feel ashamed, "but no, it was determination. I wanted Jack, so I stepped up and had him."

Diana let out a snorting laugh at the double-entendre, then clapped a hand over her mouth. "I'm so sorry," she whispered.

"No, I mean that too," Bianca said in a confiding

voice, glancing between Diana and Bea. "And that's where you have the advantage over me."

Bianca leaned in, and Bea couldn't help but crowd closer to her. She, Bianca, and Diana formed a secretive circle beside the table.

"Seduction is a tool that can be used by women just as easily as men have always used it," Bianca said. "And aren't we always saying that women should have equal rights to men?"

"We are," Diana agreed, a wicked grin spreading across her face.

"So use your best assets," Bianca went on, glancing to Bea. "Harrison is too much of a gentleman to refuse to marry you if he's compromised you in any way."

"But I couldn't lure him into that sort of a situation," Bea whispered, then blinked. "Could I?" In fact, the prospect of seducing Harrison was as appealing to her as it was shocking.

"Desperate times call for desperate measures," Bianca said, straightening. "I believe you are perfectly capable of proving too much for Harrison to resist. All you have to do is arrange the right situation, and, as the French say, *voila*!" She took a step back, spreading her hands as though she'd completed a magic trick, victory in her eyes.

"I suppose I could invite him over for supper tonight, though it's painfully short notice," Bea said, shocked that she was actually entertaining the idea.

"Short notice or no notice at all, I'd wager Harrison

would fly to your doorstep if you so much as crooked your finger," Bianca said.

Bea hoped she was right. "Papa and Evelyn will be dining at Uncle Gregory's house tonight," she went on, a plan forming in her mind. "I was going to have supper with Diana—"

"But I would gladly cede the evening to your nefarious plots, if that's what would make you happy," Diana finished her sentence for her. "Just because I don't care for the company Harrison keeps doesn't mean I'm not all in favor of you getting what you want."

Bianca made a sound as though she didn't believe a word of Diana's protest against John, but she was wise enough not to voice her opinions. "It's settled, then," she said instead. "You'll invite Harrison over for a private supper tonight, and if things progress beyond the dining room and into the bedroom—" She shrugged, grinning. "Well, all is fair in love and war, is it not?"

"I suppose it is," Bea said, excitement swirling through her. She was the last woman in London who was capable of planning and executing a seduction, but if it was the only way to prompt Harrison into making a declaration he should have made months ago, she would do it.

CHAPTER 3

y that evening, Bea was convinced that her plan was a terrible idea.

She paced the front parlor, dressed in her most gossamer, low-cut gown of pale green in a shade that complimented her unique hair color, wringing her hands. The house was empty, but for Cook and one of the footmen. After her father and younger sister had left for their supper engagement, Bea had given the rest of the upstairs staff the night off, though whether she had the authority to do that, she wasn't sure. The remaining footman had set the dining room table for two, a clever spark in his eyes that said he knew precisely what Bea was up to but wasn't going to tell a soul, and retreated back to the butler's pantry to wait until he was needed.

The clock on the mantle in the parlor ticked away, seeming as loud as a cannon with no other sound in the house and nothing to distract Bea. It was half seven. The note she'd sent to Harrison, begging him to come quickly as she needed his assistance with a delicate matter, had been sent at five o'clock. He should have been there by now. Even if the lad who had been dispatched with the letter had had a difficult time locating Harrison, he should have arrived. Perhaps she was wrong after all and Harrison didn't care for her the way she—

The grand doorbell that her father had insisted on installing several years ago gonged loudly, and Bea's heart leapt in her chest. She started toward the front hall, paused as she neared a mirror and veered off to the side to check her reflection, patted her hair, pinched her cheeks to give them color—not that she needed any more than anxiety had already given her—and skittered to the large front door to open it.

Harrison stood on the other side, his brow knit in concern, the clothes he'd worn that morning at the hall in Clerkenwell looking slightly rumpled and worse for wear. He had his hand raised to knock on the door, but at the first sight of Bea, his expression flashed to surprise and he lowered his hand. A moment later, the shock in his eyes was replaced by warmth.

"Bea." He spoke her name as if it were a benediction. His gaze raked her from bonnet to toe, and his smile widened. "You look lovely." One blink, and he was back to being confused and concerned again. "Heavens, Bea. Why are you answering the door and not Pettigrew? Is everything all right?"

He stepped through the door into the hall, and Bea moved to shut the door behind him. Her heart thundered against her ribs, and her mind was scattered with contradictory thoughts. She was so bold and daring to invite Harrison over for a seduction. She was a ninny for thinking she could pull it off. He must think her a colossal fool. He thought she looked lovely.

"Papa and Evelyn are out," she said, hovering near the door, not certain how to proceed. "I...I found myself all alone for supper, and...." She bit her lip, scrambling for a viable excuse for sending a note with the urgency of the one she'd sent. "And I thought I heard a strange noise in the house."

"What kind of a noise?" Harrison's back went straight and his expression grew protective. He looked every bit the knight she would have loved to have rescue her if there truly had been an emergency. "And where are the servants?"

"They have the night off," she said, clasping her hands in front of her and trying not to be too obvious in her lies. Though that wasn't truly a lie.

"On a Wednesday?" Harrison blinked. A moment later, his bafflement melted into a smile. That smile was amused at first, but quickly began to heat. "And you're all alone at home?"

Part of Bea wanted to thank her lucky stars that Harrison had caught on to her ruse. The rest of her was terrified...because he'd caught on to her ruse.

"Supper is ready, but I have no one to dine with," she

said in a small voice, feeling as though she were moving a piece across a chessboard.

"Well," Harrison said, removing his hat and placing it on a stand near the door, then unbuttoning his heavy, wool coat. "We wouldn't want you to have to dine alone when there are strange noises in the house."

It was all Bea could do not to giggle as she watched Harrison hang his coat, then beckoned for him to follow her into the dining room. He was as handsome in clothes worn from the day and in need of a shave as he was dressed to the nines for a society ball. And he had such an easy way with her, as though the two of them were meant to be alone together always. She only wished she felt the same ease. Unlike some of her friends, Bea had always considered herself a model of virtue and propriety. To upset that applecart now was as startling as it was thrilling.

"What took you so long to arrive?" she asked, instantly wanting to kick herself for sounding rude, as Harrison held her chair for her at the dining room table.

The smooth, almost conspiratorial look Harrison wore shuttered. "I...er...that is to say...." He cleared his throat and took the seat diagonally from her at the table— a seat that was usually reserved for her father. As soon as he'd pulled his chair into the table, Evan, the footman, stepped out of the butler's pantry to serve them wine. "I was delayed at one of the orphanages," Harrison finished his answer.

Bea blinked. "One of the orphanages?"

"Yes." Harrison seemed extraordinarily cagey about the fact. He nodded his thanks to Evan as his wine was poured, then took a long draught once Evan stepped away. Bea itched with curiosity to know why something so simple and ordinary as volunteering at an orphanage—which they'd all been doing in advance of Bianca's party on Christmas Eve—would cause him such discomfort.

Harrison was slow to answer, so Bea asked, "Which one?" simply to keep the conversation going. The evening was not turning into the seduction that she thought it would.

"Hope Orphanage," Harrison answered. "It's in Hackney." He offered nothing else.

"I assume they are one of the establishments Bianca has invited to the party?" Bea fidgeted with one of the spoons at her place, desperate to swing the conversation back to something even remotely conducive to ending the evening with Harrison in her bed and a proposal between them.

"They are," Harrison said. He cleared his throat and took another gulp of wine, glancing around the otherwise empty room. "John and I had, er, particular business there," he went on.

"Oh. John." Bea grinned, imagining what Diana would say about that. "He is a rascal," she said, some of the tension leaving her shoulders as Evan came around with the soup course. "I suppose the two of you were up to something sneaky?"

"Sneaky?" Harrison laughed a little too suddenly and

a little too loud. "Why would you say that? A gentleman is never sneaky."

"No?" Bea's smile grew. Harrison was uncomfortable for some reason. It was a rather delightful feeling to know that she had him on the back foot. It gave her a sense of power, a sense that she could take the evening in any direction she wanted.

The conversation halted until Evan had served the soup and moved back to a concealed position. Bea consumed a few spoonfuls of her soup before launching into things again.

"Your mission at Hope Orphanage must have been vital indeed to keep you and John away from your club for an afternoon," she said.

Harrison's face splashed with red, and he grinned at her. "Believe me, my dear. When the time comes, I will reveal all. Needless to say, what John and I were doing at Hope Orphanage is of vital importance." A moment later, his brow furrowed. "Though I didn't find was I was looking for."

"No?" Bea asked.

"Not yet." His smile returned. "But rest assured, I will find it eventually."

"And what were you looking for?" she asked.

Again, Harrison's expression snapped to wariness, and he didn't seem to be able to meet her eyes. "It was, um, nothing of great importance." As soon as he finished, he practically dove into his soup and ended the conversation.

His behavior puzzled Bea to the point of driving her to distraction. But being perplexed over Harrison's odd behavior wasn't what the evening was supposed to be about. She needed to find a way to steer his thoughts toward more forbidden topics. Not that she had the first idea how to do that.

"I'm so pleased that Bianca invited us all to help with her orphan cause," she tried. "I've been so impressed with the work she's done since marrying Jack Craig. Marriage seems to agree with all of our friends, don't you think?" She finished her question by lifting a last spoonful of soup to her lips and gazing at Harrison with doe eyes.

She was certainly not an accomplished flirt, but the look seemed to do the trick. Harrison nearly dropped his spoon as he raised it to his lips. Instead of finishing his soup, he set his spoon aside and gazed longingly at Bea.

"You truly do look lovely this evening," he said, heat in his eyes. "When I first saw you at the door, I thought I was seeing an angel."

"I'm hardly that," Bea said, her insides fluttering. She lowered her eyes enough to be able to send him what she hoped was a sensual look and leaned slightly toward him.

Evan chose that moment to reenter the room so that he could take their soup bowls away. Bea snapped straight, inwardly telling herself to behave. Though Bianca's voice in her mind instantly told her that behaving herself was precisely what she shouldn't be doing that evening. She and Harrison sat in stiff silence until Evan brought out the main course—blessedly already arranged on their plates in the style of a restaurant—then retreated to the shadows once again.

"I am very much looking forward to Christmas Eve," Bea started up the conversation again as both she and Harrison sliced into their roast. "I've been looking forward to the magical moment for a long time."

Harrison nearly choked on the bite he'd just taken. "How...how did you know?"

Bea was so startled by his reaction that she nearly swallowed her own bite wrong. "Know?"

"About...about Christmas Eve," Harrison said, fidgeting with his fork.

"It happens every year at roughly the same time," Bea said with a burst of humor. "And the May Flowers have been planning the benefit for Bianca's cause for over a month now. Well, half of the May Flowers. We won't talk about Lady Claudia's cabal."

"Oh." Harrison let out a breath of relief that had Bea more confused than ever. "The orphan event. Of course."

"What did you think I meant?" Bea asked, wondering what had gotten into Harrison. But, of course, it was obvious. She'd ambushed him with supper and seduction. He must have sensed that they were about to cross the Rubicon into a whole different level of their friendship.

"I...I assumed you meant the orphan event, of course," he said, sawing his roast as though it had offended him, though Bea suspected that was merely a way for him not to have to meet her eyes.

The whole evening was taking a turn for the decidedly strange. She had to focus and bring things back around to where she wanted them. Proposal. That was her aim. Spending the rest of her days with Harrison as his wife. Getting there by using her feminine wiles. Though, if she were honest with herself, she wasn't sure how many feminine wiles she actually possessed.

"Harrison, there is something I have wanted to say to you for so very long now," she said, forcing herself to be bold.

"Yes?" He leaned toward her, expectation and affection in his eyes.

Bea took a breath, steeling her courage. "I do so love —" she gulped, losing her nerve at the very last moment. "Christmas," she finished with a croak, feeling her face heat. "I do so love Christmas."

"So do I," he said, his smile widening. "It's been one of my favorite holidays since I was a boy." He paused, then reached across the corner of the table to take her hand. Bea's pulse sped up to the point of making her feel dizzy. "Christmas is the perfect time of year for...for declarations of a...a particular sort."

"Yes, it is," she agreed breathlessly. It was coming. She could feel it. The proposal she'd longed for was just on the other side of Harrison's lips.

"Bea," he said, gazing earnestly into her eyes. "I was wondering if you would—"

Evan stepped around the screen shielding the

butler's pantry and came forward to refill their wine glasses. Immediately, Bea snapped straight, lowering her head guiltily and focusing on cutting her potatoes.

Harrison shifted back to his place as well. "This roast is delicious," he told Evan as the young man topped off his wine glass. "Please give my compliments to the cook."

"Yes, my lord," Evan said, then headed back to the butler's pantry.

For the briefest of moments, Bea thought that perhaps she could hear the soft giggling of one or more of the maids. She put the possibility out of her mind, though, unable to contemplate that on top of everything else.

"I was thinking of wearing this gown to the party on Christmas Eve," she said, though she'd been thinking no such thing. She didn't think she could bear the silence that Evan's interruption had brought with it, though.

"It's a simply divine gown," Harrison said, studying her with an increasingly amorous grin. "But I'm not certain it's appropriate for a party in Clerkenwell."

"No?" Bea took the opportunity to shift her chair back and stand. She stepped away from the table and executed a quick turn that flared the soft fabric of her skirt. "I thought it was perfect for a Christmas party."

"It is," Harrison said, standing as well. "But one in Mayfair, not Clerkenwell." He took half a step closer to her, studying her.

Bea felt her moment to act. "You don't think it's too

revealing?" she asked, brushing her hand along the low neckline.

"I—" Harrison started, but seemed to lose his train of thought. "I think it suits you beautifully," he said, his voice hoarse.

The tension in the air between them was almost unbearable, but in the most delicious of ways. Bea knew she had to act. If she was going to live up to the example her friends had set for her and grab onto her happiness with both hands, she had to be bolder than she'd ever been before. She was ready. She could do it. She would dive into the breach with—

Before she could finish talking herself into action, Harrison stepped into her, resting his hands on her waist. He leaned in, slanting his mouth over hers and drinking in a kiss that had her head spinning and her heart racing. His lips tasted of wine and herbs, which encouraged her all the more to open to him and let him slide his tongue along hers. She'd never been kissed at all before and was delighted to discover there was more to it than simply lips bussing lips.

She made a noise deep in her throat and slid her arms over Harrison's shoulders, losing her fingers in his hair. She'd never touched his hair before and was thrilled to discover how soft it was. It was a delicious contrast to the firmness of his chest against hers and the strength in his arms as he pulled her closer and deepened his kiss. If this was seduction, she couldn't get enough of it, whether he started it or her. All she wanted to do was lose herself in Harrison's kiss, and he seemed more than happy oblige.

"My darling," he murmured against her lips, teasing her cheek and the top of her neck with feather-light kisses. "You know I adore you. I love—"

"What on earth is the meaning of this?"

Her father's booming voice from the doorway to the dining room had Bea feeling as though she'd been struck by lightning. She yelped and jumped away from Harrison, nearly toppling over as she did.

"Papa," she gasped once she had her footing. "You're home." Her face burned so hot with guilt at being caught in an embrace with Harrison that she rivaled the fire crackling in the fireplace.

"Your sister felt unwell," her father said, sauntering deeper into the room. His expression was as grave and ferocious as a lion, but if Bea wasn't mistaken, there was a measure of humor in his eyes. "Landsbury." He nodded to Harrison, the single word spoken as a pure challenge.

"My lord," Harrison gulped. He cleared his throat and stood as straight as he could, tugging at the hem of his coat and doing everything in his power to look like the marquess he was. "Let me explain."

"There is no need to explain," Bea's father said in an ominous voice. "When the cat is away for the evening, the mice play. Is that not right, my dear?" he asked Bea.

"I...I invited Harrison for supper because...because I did not want to eat alone," Bea fumbled, knowing there was no chance her father would believe her. "He was...

we were…I was choking on a piece of roast." The lie fell clumsily from her lips, and she clapped a hand over her mouth once it was out.

The corner of her father's mouth twitched. He sent a pointed glance to Harrison. "You've saved my daughter's life this evening, then?"

Bea had the distinct impression her father was teasing them, but Harrison answered. "It would appear so."

Her father hummed. "I see. Well, then, young man. I expect to see you in my office at your earliest possible convenience so that we can discuss a reward for you saving my dear Beatrice's life."

"Understood, my lord," Harrison said with a sharp bow, looking more embarrassed than proud of his deeds. He flinched, then said, "I have a matter of great importance that I need to see to on the morrow, though."

"Oh?" Bea's father arched one eyebrow at him.

"Yes," Harrison went on. "It is a matter that requires swift action before…before something is lost permanently. By your leave, may I come speak to you once the item I've been searching for is recovered?"

Bea's father stared at him for a moment, then sighed and said, "As long as you don't change your mind."

"Never, sir," Harrison said, sending Bea a sideways look. He cleared his throat. "Now, if you will excuse me, I'm afraid I've overstayed my welcome this evening."

Bea wanted to call after him not to go, but considering she'd invited him there without her father's knowledge or permission, and relatively certain she was about to be told off for doing so, she didn't try to stop him. But one, shining bit of hope remained with her, even after Harrison was gone. If her father didn't believe her lie, if he was intent on speaking with Harrison soon, then perhaps a proposal would come out of the whole thing after all.

# CHAPTER 4

"It was mortifying," Bea whispered to Diana and Phoebe Long as they cut squares of wrapping paper for the gifts that had been donated to give to the mountain of orphans that would be at the Christmas Eve party. "Papa walked in, and there Harrison and I were. Kissing."

"I don't know what I would have done," Phoebe said, her eyes round. "It's bad enough that my mother has stumbled across Danny and I kissing once or twice since we've been married, but to have one's father interrupt a kiss with a beau?" She made a horrified sound as if to prove how alarming that would be.

"The worst part of it all was that it was my very first kiss," Bea said with a wistful sigh. She would remember that kiss—before her father interrupted them—for the rest of her life. It was everything she'd dreamed a kiss would be—tender, passionate, and overwhelming in the happiest of ways. There was no telling how long it would have gone on or where it would have led if it hadn't been interrupted.

"You and Lord Landsbury truly hadn't kissed before that?" Phoebe asked carefully.

Bea didn't know Phoebe as well as her other friends. She was a relatively late admission to their friend circle. She'd just married Danny Long, who was a friend of the male part of their group. In spite of having been born working class, Mr. Long was a property developer and currently one of the wealthiest men in London. The London papers were all calling it a coup of the highest order that he had snagged the daughter of a marquess for his bride, and lauding Phoebe as a genius for marrying a diamond in the rough. From what Bea had heard, theirs was actually a love match, something she aspired to.

"We'd never kissed, no," Bea confessed, inwardly calling herself a ninny for being so bashful about something she hadn't done. "I suppose we had never found ourselves in a situation where such a thing would have been possible until last night."

"And Bianca encouraged you to seduce Harrison," Diana said with a snorting laugh.

Phoebe's eyes went wide as she glanced from Diana to Bea. "Was that your plan?"

"It was," Bea admitted, her face and neck heating. She shook her head. "Though looking back at the way things turned out, that whole plan represented gross over-confidence on my part."

"How so?" Phoebe asked with a look of curiosity as she wrapped a rag doll in bright pink paper printed with holly.

"I'm not that sort of woman," Bea admitted.

A mysterious grin flittered across Phoebe's beautiful face. "I didn't think I was that sort of woman either," she said with a mischievous lift of her brow.

Bea giggled before she could stop to think whether it was appropriate. Diana laughed much more freely than her.

"You'd never catch me seducing a man or letting myself be seduced," she said.

"Oh, really?" Bianca walked up to check on their work at just that moment. She sent Diana a sardonic grin as she overheard the comment.

Diana stiffened her back proudly. "I choose to imitate my namesake," she said. "No man will win my favors without a good fight."

"I'll tell Lord John you said that," Bianca said with a smirk, then glanced over their shoulders to take a look at their work. "I've never seen so many toys in need of wrapping in my life," she said. "But you're all doing a fine job."

"Your orphans will be overjoyed by their good fortune," Bea said, reaching for a wooden boat to wrap in blue paper. "I'm certain the men and women who run each and every one of the orphanages that will be receiving your charity are eternally grateful."

"I certainly hope they are," Bianca said with a sudden sigh. When Bea glanced curiously at her, Bianca went on with, "There was another incident at an orphanage yesterday."

"Oh?" Phoebe asked.

All three of them stopped what they were doing to turn to Bianca.

"As if the incident with the treacle destroying a bunch of books at St. Joseph's wasn't bad enough, someone replaced all of the sugar at Hope Orphanage with salt," Bianca said.

A strange tightness gripped Bea's gut. "Hope Orphanage?" she asked. She was certain that was the name of the place Harrison said he'd been before receiving her invitation to supper and joining her.

"Yes," Bianca said. "It's in Hackney. And it's one of the hardest cases of any that we're working with."

"Oh, my," Phoebe said, pressing a hand to her stomach. "And sugar is such a dear commodity."

"One that children seem to go through faster than anyone else," Diana said, though there was far more suspicion in her frown than the thought of children and sugar warranted.

"If Hope Orphanage needs its sugar replaced," Phoebe started, "indeed, if they need more, if they need sweets or treats of any sort, I know that Danny and I would be more than willing to donate to the cause."

"I'm certain the children and the proprietors of Hope Orphanage would be more than happy for your offer," Bianca said. She frowned and reached for a sheet of colorful paper and one of the toys in need of wrapping.

"Two pranks at two orphanages in two days," she said as she set to work. "I know that it's Christmastime and everyone is in high spirits, but it seems a bit cruel to play jokes when so much else is going on."

"It sounds like precisely the sort of thing that men who don't care what others think would do," Diana said, narrowing her eyes with the look she only wore when speaking or thinking about John.

"It sounds like the sort of thing children would do," Bea attempted to correct where she was certain Diana's thoughts were heading.

Diana didn't answer her, either to refute or agree with Bea's assessment. That left an opening for Bianca to turn to Bea and ask, "And how did your evening go, Lady Beatrice?"

The heat of embarrassment flooded Bea's face all over again. "It didn't go," she confessed in a quiet voice. "At least, not the way you would have wanted it to."

"No seduction, then?" Bianca asked in a carelessly loud voice. "No proposal?"

Bea wanted to shush her. She glanced around desperately, praying that no one was listening in. "No," she whispered. "But there was a kiss."

"Oh?" Bianca burst into a saucy smile. "A good one, I hope."

"Very good." The memory of it swirled through Bea, tickling her heart. "But Papa interrupted it."

"I thought your father was supposed to be out for the evening," Bianca said.

"He was, but he and my sister returned home early."

"How early? I thought Harrison was supposed to be at your house shortly after they departed," Bianca pushed the matter.

"Harrison was delayed," Bea said. She glanced to Diana, dreading what she was about to say because she knew exactly what her friend would do with the information. "He and John were on some sort of mission to search for something at Hope Orphanage."

Sure enough, Diana gasped and dropped the gift she was wrapping. "*He* was at Hope Orphanage?" she asked, predictably. There was no possible way to think that by "he" Diana meant Harrison.

"Yes," Bea said, raising a hand to caution her friend, "But I doubt there's any correlation."

"I knew it," Diana said all the same. "That's just the sort of nefarious deed John would get up to. Only a man of his low character would play pranks on orphanages at Christmas."

"You think John and Harrison are responsible?" Bianca asked, amusement sharp in her eyes.

"I know it," Diana said. "Just wait. I bet they'll tip their hands and expose themselves before the day is done."

"I think you must be mistaken," Bea said, then quickly rushed on with, "I'm just going to take these wrapped gifts over to the tree so Mrs. Coldwell can arrange them."

Anything to get away from Diana and her mad

vendetta against John. Although Bea did find the ferocity of Diana's feelings toward John to be good fun. At least, she did when she wasn't too busy mired in her own problems. She heaved a wistful sigh as she carried a basket of wrapped dolls, toy soldiers, wooden vehicles, and soft animals across the room to one of the row of Christmas trees that had been erected on either side of the room's largest fireplace. She heartily approved of the relatively new tradition of bringing pine trees indoors and decorating them. She handed the basket of toys off to the no-nonsense Mrs. Coldwell, who was organizing the middle-class women who had come to help, then took a step back to admire the trees.

Her backward step sent her crashing right into a solid body. She yelped and whipped around in surprise, only to find herself face-to-face with Harrison. He still wore his wool coat and hat, and his face was pink, as though he'd walked through the bitter cold of the London streets to reach the hall.

"Oh, I'm terribly sorry," Bea said, her gaze fluttering down even as heat rose within her. She couldn't quite bring herself to look into Harrison's eyes. Not after the way things had gone between the two of them the night before, not with his kiss still tingling on her lips.

"It was my fault, I'm sure," Harrison said, his eyes bright with a smile as he stared at her. "I should have watched where I was going." His gaze settled on her lips, and his smile grew.

"I've been such a ninny today," Bea prattled on. "So

distracted and...." She realized too late that she'd raised a hand to touch her lips as Harrison stared at them.

"Yes, I know," he said with a far-off softness in his voice. A moment later, he sucked in a breath and shook himself. "I mean...that is to say...the fault is all mine, I'm sure."

For a moment, they just stood there, staring at each other. Part of Bea was perfectly content just to be in Harrison's presence. The rest of her felt beyond awkward, as if she'd created the awkward situation but didn't have the first clue what to do about it.

Harrison's mind had gone completely blank except for the single thought, "Do something, you twat."

All he could think about as he gazed at Bea's beautiful, innocent face was that he had better find his great-grandmother's ring before the moment when he had to face Bea's father so that he could prove to the man that marriage had been his intention all along. It had been mortifying to be caught compromising Bea. He would rather have died than do anything to her that might damage her reputation. In a way, it was a blessing that his momentary lapse of reason had come in the privacy of Bea's own home—although he'd been fairly certain the servants had been spying on them—so that she was spared public humiliation. But in another way, it was so much worse that they had been caught by her father.

Those thoughts were eclipsed by the realization that

he was standing in the middle of a public hall filled with people, staring dumbly at the woman he loved but couldn't seem to do right by.

"I came looking for John," he blurted at last. "Have you seen him?"

Bea blinked and shook herself, peeking around at the room filled mostly with women. "No, not yet." She paused and the most charming grin passed over her lips as she went on with, "I'm sure Diana would have alerted me to his presence if he were here."

Harrison caught her grin and returned it. "They are ridiculous, aren't they?"

"Very." Bea giggled, clapping a hand over her mouth.

For one, wild moment, Harrison wished he were that hand. It would have been heaven to touch her lips again, to kiss her with all the passion that had been interrupted the night before. With any luck, as soon as he found the ring and proposed in a way that Bea deserved, they would have their rest of their lives to kiss each other.

Another moment passed, and Bea lowered her hand, smiling at something past Harrison's shoulder. "There he is now," she said, nodding in the direction of the door.

Sure enough, John had arrived. He spotted Harrison and nodded as he walked toward him. He also glanced across the room and winked at Diana when she looked up from her work. The color that came to Diana's face and the fury in her eyes was enough to set Harrison laughing. There was a very fine line between love and hate.

"Morning, Harrison," John said when he arrived. He turned to Bea. "You're looking lovely today, Bea."

"Thank you, John." Bea smiled under the compliment, glanced to Harrison, then said, "I'd better get back to work."

She dashed off before Harrison could say a proper goodbye, before he could tell her any of the things he wanted to, like how sorry he was for putting her in an awkward position with her father or how desperately he loved her.

"Ah, the lovesick puppy look," John chuckled, slapping Harrison's shoulder and snapping him out of his reverie. "Did you decide to go ahead and propose last night without the ring?"

Harrison turned to his friend, nodding toward the door. They headed out of the hall. John had been with Harrison the evening before when he'd received Bea's note that she needed him, so he knew the beginnings of the story.

"She invited me to supper," he filled John in on the rest of it as they left the building.

"That was the emergency?" John laughed. "Supper?"

Harrison sent him a flat, sideways look. "I suspect the emergency was an invention. Her father and sister were out for the evening."

"Oh?" John's brow shot all the way up and he laughed. "What a cunning little minx you have on your hands."

Their conversation was halted as Burt leapt up from

the front stairs of the hall and bounded over to meet them. "My lords," he said, doffing his cap. "I'm ready to lead you on to the second orphanage."

"Good lad," John said, taking a coin from his pocket and flicking it toward Burt. It made a satisfying sound as John's nail hit it, and Burt caught it with a grin.

"You won't be disappointed," Burt said. "I'm sure whatever you're looking for is at Mr. Stephen Siddel's place in Limehouse. Follow me. It'll be easier to hail a cab at the end of the street." The lad looked beyond happy at the prospect of riding in a cab to Limehouse instead of having to walk.

"Bea's plan for an evening alone would have been perfectly delightful," Harrison continued as he and John strolled after Burt, "had her father and sister not returned home early and caught us with our lips locked together."

John laughed outright. "And how did you wheedle out of that situation without ending up engaged on the spot?"

"I'm not sure I did," Harrison said, his embarrassment from the night before making a pointed return. "Lord Lichfield wants to speak with me as soon as possible. But what an ignominious way to get precisely what I want. Forced into it by Bea's father."

"It would hardly be forcing anything, if you ask me," John said, nodding to Burt, who had caught the attention of a cab once they reached the curb. "You've wanted to marry Bea for almost as long as you've known her."

"Yes, but being cornered into it because of a momen-

51

tary lapse of judgement is hardly the most romantic way to go about the thing."

"True," John agreed.

"There's nothing for it but to find my great-grand-mother's ring as quickly as possible so that I can propose to Bea properly," Harrison said as the carriage pulled up to the curb in front of them. "Otherwise, I run the risk of Bea forever wondering whether marrying her was my idea or her father's."

"Here you go, my lords," Burt said, grabbing the carriage's door and holding it open for them, as if he had aspirations of being a doorman at a grand hotel someday.

"Surely she knows you love her," John said, giving Burt a wink and rubbing his head, then hopping into the carriage.

"I hope so," Harrison said, climbing in behind John. Burt leapt in with them and shut the door, looking as happy as a clam to be riding in a carriage with two gentle-men. "Either way, it all comes down to time and the ring. We have to find it so I can give Bea what she deserves."

CHAPTER 5

"Oh! Did you see that?" Diana hissed, glaring at the doorway Harrison and John had just rushed out through and stomping her foot. "Why, I've never been so insulted in my life."

Bea blinked up from the gift she was wrapping and glanced from the doorway to Diana. She did her best to keep her sly grin from growing too big, but one covert glance to Bianca and her efforts failed. She and Bianca were giggling before they knew it.

"Did I miss something?" Phoebe asked, the only one of them who looked confused by the turn of events. "What has happened to insult you?"

"John swans into the hall, as if he hasn't a care in the world, winks at me, and doesn't have the decency to come over here to address me face to face," Diana sniffed, tilting her chin up.

"It looked as though he and Harrison were merely

meeting here, but that they have business elsewhere," Bea said.

The thought switched her from laughing at Diana to furrowing her brow in thought. What sort of business could Harrison and John have so close to Christmas? Could it be possible that after the debacle of the evening before, he was planning the proposal she'd waited so long for? But no, he'd informed her father that he already had business to attend to, business he had contracted before the kiss the night before ever happened, which was why he was unavailable to meet with her father. She was struck with sudden worry about what that business could be.

"Still," Diana went on, "it was unforgivably rude for him not to at least say hello."

Bianca laughed so hard she snorted, which had Bea breaking into a smile again.

"I'm sorry, I still don't understand what's going on," Phoebe said, finishing with the box of toy soldiers she'd wrapped and reaching for another one.

"My dearest friends are laughing at me," Diana said in a flat voice, though she was amused enough by Bea and Bianca's carrying on to smirk.

"Do you love him or hate him?" Bianca asked with an impatient sigh.

"I hate him," Diana insisted, her back snapping straight.

"Then why do you care that he didn't come over here to greet us?" Bianca shook her head as though Diana were impossible. "Never mind," she went on. "It looks as though we're about to finish wrapping all of these gifts. Phoebe can finish up with the last of them. I'm certain more will come in today and tomorrow, but in the meantime, I have a different sort of errand I was hoping the two of you would run." She glanced to Bea and Diana.

Bea tied the last bow on the gift she'd finished wrapping as her thoughts wandered. "I'm at your disposal," she said with a shrug.

Bianca gestured for her and Diana to follow her around the table and over to the side of the room where several large baskets of freshly-baked bread, rolls, and cakes were waiting on a table. "We've had so many generous donations, but if we let things like this sit around until Christmas Eve, they'll be pitifully stale by the time we hand them out. I need you to take this lot down to Limehouse, to Stephen Siddel's orphanage."

"Limehouse?" Diana's expression lit with adventure. "That's not the sort of place one finds oneself every day."

"There's nothing wrong with Limehouse," Bianca sighed. "And there's nothing wrong with the working class." She picked up one of the baskets, thrusting it into Diana's arms. "I'm certain John wouldn't like it if he thought you were too proud to venture into a working-class neighborhood."

"I am not—" Diana sputtered, juggling the basket to get a better hold on it. "I would never—" She gave up her protests with a sigh. "Bea and I would be more than happy to take these things to Limehouse."

55

Bea watched the whole interchange with an amused grin. Diana was one of the least snobbish ladies she knew, but her feud with John had her in high spirits. They were likely to have quite the adventure in Limehouse.

She lifted one of the baskets and looped it over her arm, then accepted a few coins from Bianca to pay for their cab fare. She and Diana made their way out to the street, laden with baked goods, and managed to hail one of the carriages that was lurking near the end of the street. The driver likely knew that a passel of aristocrats were hard at work on the orphan event and that they would need transportation.

"I, for one, will be overjoyed to have this entire thing over with," Diana sighed as the carriage made its way into Limehouse, to the address for Stephen Siddel's orphanage.

Bea couldn't contain her smile. They'd chattered about this and that for the entire trip, but it was only a matter of time before her friend said something that opened the gates for more teasing.

"Yes, I think we'll all be overjoyed when the feud finally stops and you and John fall into each other's arms, like we all know you're going to," she said as the driver held the door open for them to disembark.

"That's not what I meant," Diana said with a sharp stare. She stepped down from the carriage, then turned to fetch the baskets. "I meant that I'll be grateful after the party, after we've made innumerable orphans happy and given them a delightful Christmas. I simply cannot wait to put my feet up for days on end after Christmas is over."

Bea's humor took a solemn turn and she sighed. "I was so hoping that I would be spending this Christmas celebrating more than our Lord's birth."

The door to the orphanage stood open, so she and Diana walked right in with their baskets after paying the cab driver.

"You may still have something to celebrate," Diana said with surprising compassion.

Stephen Siddel's orphanage was everything Bea would have expected from an overcrowded, underfunded orphanage in Limehouse. The building itself was sound and the hall they entered was clean, but the entire place was decidedly shabby. Pegs lined the wall in the front hall that were hung with mismatched, threadbare wool coats and the simplest hats imaginable. Just off of the hall-ways was a vast room that looked to be a dining room and activity hall rolled into one. Several long rows of tables with benches ran the length of the room with a shorter table placed perpendicularly to the rest at the front of the room. The wallpaper was faded to the point where Bea wasn't certain what color it was supposed to be, but the walls were decorated with paper snowflakes and other decorations that must have been made by the girls who called the orphanage home. Several of them sat at the tables, working on schoolwork or needlework or making more Christmas decorations. Bea found the whole thing charming, but slightly sad.

"Hello, ladies. Can I help you?"

Bea and Diana turned to the attractive young man with spectacles who walked into the room behind them. He had an air of kindness about him that immediately put Bea at ease, even though he was dressed in clothes that didn't look much finer than the things the girls wore. To Bea, that was a good sign. It meant the man put his charges ahead of his own needs. For there was no mistaking that the man was the proprietor of the orphanage, in spite of the fact that he wasn't much older than Bea.

"Are you Mr. Siddel?" Diana asked with a gracious smile.

"I am." Mr. Siddel immediately reached for the basket in her arms, as if his first and only concern was to take the heavy burden from her. "You must be with the May Flowers."

"We are," Bea said, instantly adoring the man as much as the girls who glanced up from their work to smile at him obviously did. One of the smaller girls even left her table to walk up to Mr. Siddel's side and take hold of the hem of his jacket. "I am Lady Beatrice Lichfield, and this is Lady Diana Pickwick."

Mr. Siddel's smile brightened. "Forgive me for not greeting you more formally, my ladies," he said with a slight bow.

"We don't stand on ceremony," Diana said. "We were sent to bring you these things for immediate consumption."

"Lady Clerkenwell doesn't want them to go stale before they're eaten," Bea added.

The girls in the hall had all perked up and were looking on with interest. Mr. Siddel seemed to be fully aware of the fact.

"Let's all take a look at what we've been given, shall we?" he asked, taking the basket he carried to the nearest table.

A commotion erupted as the girls leapt up from their tasks to crowd around the table where Mr. Siddel and Bea set the baskets and started emptying the contents.

"Mmm. This bread smells good," one of the girls said.

"Are those hot cross buns?" another asked.

"Not at Christmas," an older girl answered. "Hot cross buns are for Easter."

"Is there any plum pudding?" another older girl asked.

"No, but look at how pretty this cake is," another answered her.

Bea grinned from ear to ear, touched by how a simple basket of treats could bring so much joy to so many girls. It made her reconsider the things she thought were so important in her life.

"Let's have some things now, but save most of it for later," Mr. Siddel said, distributing small scones with sultanas to the girls crowding around him. "Annie, would you mind taking these two baskets to your mother in the kitchen?"

A young woman who was just slightly older than the

oldest orphans stepped forward. She gazed at Mr. Siddel with absolute adoration as she reached for one of the baskets. "Yes, Mr. Siddel," she said in a smitten voice.

Bea glanced to Diana. Annie was as obvious as Diana was in her regard for a man. "We can help you," she said, taking up the basket she'd just put on the table. "It's too much of a load for one person to manage on their own."

"Oh, but the kitchens," Annie said, her eyes wide. "And you being ladies."

"Kitchens never did any harm to ladies," Diana said, lifting one of the other baskets into her arms.

They left the third basket and its contents on the table for Mr. Siddel to sort out and marched out of the room and down the hallway, following Annie.

"Mama will be so pleased to receive this bounty," Annie chattered as they passed a few rooms that appeared to be schoolrooms. "She's always at her wit's end when it comes to—"

The rumble of male voices wafting down the stairs at the end of the hall caught Bea completely by surprise. She would recognize Harrison's voice anywhere, and John with him.

"He can't be," Diana gasped, her brow knitting into a scowl.

As Harrison and John came into view at the top of the stairs, Diana grabbed Bea's arm and dove into the nearest classroom. Before Bea knew what was going on, Diana had both of them with their backs pressed to the wall on the other side of the open door. Annie had leapt into the room with them and looked completely baffled by Diana's behavior.

"What are you doing?" Bea whispered as Harrison's and John's footsteps sounded on the stairs, growing nearer.

"The true question is what are they doing here?" Diana whispered in return.

"Do you know Lord Lichfield and Lord Whitlock?" Annie crowded against the wall with them, her eyes sparkling with the mischief she must have thought she was getting up to.

"Yes, we know them, all right," Diana said ominously. "We know them better than they know themselves."

Bea sent her friend a wary look. Her vendetta was getting a bit out of hand if it meant the two of them were crouched in hiding in a schoolroom. Although her ears did prick up at the conversation Harrison and John were engaged in as they passed the room.

"...don't know what I'm going to do," Harrison was in the middle of saying. He was clearly distressed. "Grandmama is going to have my hide for this."

"Grandmothers seldom approve of anything their grandsons do," John said as they passed right in front of the door.

Diana sank deeper into the room, dragging Bea with her, so that there was no chance the two of them would be spotted. Bea had just enough of a view to catch Harrison bending over to pick up a roll that had spilled out of one of their baskets.

"That's odd," she thought she heard him say before going on with, "I'll likely be disowned once she finds out what I've done. She's always guarded the family honor and the trappings of that honor religiously. I'll be drummed right out of the family for losing something so precious."

"I doubt it'll be as bad as all that," John said, his voice fading as the two of them walked on toward the orphanage's main room. "You can always find another one. Pretty jewels like that are available all over the city."

They stepped out of earshot, and Diana snapped straight so fast a loaf of bread spilled out of her basket. "That villain," she growled, her face like a thundercloud. "To suggest that women are jewels that can be bought and sold and replaced on a whim. Ugh!"

Bea's heart was too bruised by what she'd heard to shush her friend into silence. Did Harrison's grandmother not approve of their match? Is that why he'd taken so long to declare himself? He hadn't really declared himself in the end, he'd only kissed her. If his family didn't approve of her, no wonder Harrison was so reticent about speaking to her father.

"We aren't going to let them get away with this," Diana said, sneaking carefully out of her concealment.

"Get away with what?" Annie asked in an awed whisper.

Diana hesitated before saying, "Whatever it is they're plotting."

"I'm not certain they're plotting anything," Bea said, rubbing a hand over her sore heart.

"I'm certain they are," Diana insisted. "We'll take these things to the kitchen, then follow them to see what they're up to."

Bea sent her friend a wary, sideways look, but followed her out of the classroom and down to the kitchen, as careful as Diana was not to be seen by Harrison or John, who had disappeared, likely into the main hall. They delivered the baskets to Mrs. Ross, Annie's mother, then left the two women to sort through them as they headed to the main hall.

"We should just make ourselves known and ask why they're here," Bea said with the strong feeling that she needed to be the voice of reason where her friend was concerned.

"I'm sure they—"

Diana was cut off by a blood-curdling scream from the floor above them. A moment later, that first scream was joined by a few more. Within seconds, a stampede of girls poured down the stairs, pursued by half a dozen ferrets.

"Get away from me, get away from me," one of the girls shouted as they all spilled into the downstairs hall, dodging around Bea and Diana in their rush to the orphanage's main room.

"I think they're cute," a lone girl at the top of the stairs, who held ferrets in each hand, said.

"They are not cute, they are rodents," an older girl shouted at her.

Several more ferrets dashed down the stairs, as if chasing the girls.

Mr. Siddel darted into the hall, adjusting his glasses. "What in heaven's name is going on out here?" he asked.

"Ferrets," one of the girls moaned. "A whole, big box of them. Somebody left it in the dormitory, and when we opened it, there were dozens of ferrets everywhere."

Bea didn't know whether to laugh or scream along with the girls. She'd never been overly fond of the creatures herself, though she knew people kept them as pets. All the same, she leapt into action, helping Mr. Siddel when he gave the order to catch the animals and gather them in one spot.

"Where is the box they came in?" he asked, lunging to catch one of the slippery creatures before it could escape into the schoolroom.

"I've got it right here," a young lad—who Bea remembered seeing at the hall in Clerkenwell—said, charging down the stairs with a large crate in his arms.

Mr. Siddel nodded to the lad and pointed, ferret in his hand, toward the orphanage's main room. "We'll take them to the hall and put them all back in the box."

"Who would do something like this to us?" one of the older girls wailed, shying away from Mr. Siddel as he marched past with a handful of ferrets.

"It was them," Diana declared, as though personifying vengeance itself. She marched along the hallway and burst into the main room as if expecting to uncover a coup. Sadly for her, neither Harrison nor John were in the main room. "I know it was them," Diana raged on, searching as though the two men would materialize out of nowhere.

"Diana, I don't think Harrison and John would do such a thing," Bea said, resting a hand on her friend's arm.

"They were just here," Diana said with a calculating look. "And didn't you say that Harrison had come from Hope Orphanage before arriving, late, to your house last night? There was a prank at Hope Orphanage as well."

Bea swallowed uncomfortably. It was true. And the first prank had happened at St. Joseph's. Were Harrison and John there as well? They wouldn't possibly attempt something so childish...would they? Perhaps that was why Harrison's grandmother would disown him.

"We have to go after them," Diana said, looking like the goddess she'd been named after. "Where did they go?"

"Who, the nobs?" the lad who had brought the crate into the hall asked. When Diana turned to him, he bobbed into a bow and said, "Beggin' your pardon, my lady."

"You." Diana approached the boy. "Your name is Burt, isn't it?"

"It is, my lady," Burt said.

"Do you know where Lord Whitlock has gone?"

"I do, my lady. He and Lord Landsbury have gone up the street, to the Sisters of Perpetual Sorrow."

"Then you will take us there," Diana insisted.

Burt's face split into a grin. "Right you are, my lady."

Diana marched out of the hall without so much as a goodbye for Mr. Siddel. Bea waved to him, but that was all she could manage. They headed for the outside door, but before they could reach it, Annie dashed up the hall from the kitchen, something small in her hand.

"If you please, my lady," she called, catching up to Bea as Diana burst through the door and out into the street, led by Burt. "I have something for Lord Landsbury."

Bea blinked at the young woman in surprise. "You do?"

"Yes." Annie nodded and presented Bea with a small, linen sack that had something solid and square inside. "It was with the donations that were brought to us yesterday," Annie explained. "I heard Lord Landsbury talking to his friend earlier about how he'd misplaced something with the donations. I felt it was my duty to return it, but with so much going on today, I didn't get a chance. Will you take it to him?"

"Certainly," Bea said, accepting the parcel with a gracious smile.

"Bea!" Diana called from the doorway. "Time is wasting. We need to catch the bastards in the act."

Bea gasped at her friend's harsh language and tucked

the linen sack and its contents into the coat of her thick, wool coat. "Oh dear," she told Annie. "I mustn't delay."

Annie grinned and bobbed a curtsy as Bea turned to rush after Diana and whatever new madness awaited them.

## CHAPTER 6

"The boxes from yesterday have been taken to the sanctuary for sorting," Sister Constance informed Harrison almost as soon as he and John arrived at the orphanage run by the Sisters of Perpetual Sorrow. "You are welcome to search there, but I'm not sure you'll have any luck," the stony-faced sister informed them.

"We have to try," Harrison said, doing his best to be as deferential to the middle-aged nun as possible. "The ring has great value to my family, not to mention being of vital importance to my own endeavors."

"Vital importance," Burt repeated, as though he were the one with all the importance.

Harrison grinned at the lad. He'd been of great help in taking him and John where they needed to go. Harrison suspected the lad had grand ideas about himself and where he might end up in the world.

Sister Constance didn't seem as certain. "That's enough cheek out of you, young man."

"I'm not cheeky." Burt bristled, assuming an air of superiority that he'd probably learned through observing all of the well-born helpers Bianca had enlisted.

"You are so," John said, ruffling the boy's hair.

Burt laughed. "Well, if I am, it's because it's fun."

"Christmas is not a time for *fun*," Sister Constance insisted. "It is a time for reflection about the redemption of the world."

"It is?" Burt blinked, as though it was news to him.

"Scamp," John laughed.

"Go on with you, boy." Sister Constance sniffed. "You've led these gentlemen to our door, and now you can go on your way."

"Could I have a bit of a pop into the kitchens before I go, sister?" Burt asked.

Sister Constance sighed, shook her head, and gestured for Burt to head on deeper into the orphanage. She shook her head again once he was gone.

Harrison couldn't help but smile and wonder if Sister Constance's bad humor was all for show. "We cannot thank you enough for letting us drop in like this," he said. "This is our last hope for finding the ring I've lost."

Sister Constance hummed and crossed her arms, staring down her nose at him as though he had been woefully irresponsible to lose something so valuable. Harrison had the feeling his grandmother would look at him the same way if she knew.

"I'm afraid the sanctuary is a bit of a jumble at the moment," Sister Constance said as she led them down a long and drafty hall. "Between the wealth of donations we receive at this time of year and preparations for our own, solemn observations of Christ's birth, things are a bit up in the air."

Harrison wondered what the nun's definition of up in the air was. As far as he could see, the building that housed the Sisters of Perpetual Sorrow and their charges lived up to its name in every way. The walls were drab stone with very little adornment. The rooms that he and John passed and were able to look into had only the most meager fires in their grates. Boys and girls in grey uniforms hunched over their schoolwork, even though it was the day before Christmas Eve, or stood reciting bits of scriptures to the young novices who had been put in charge of them. There were very few glimpses of color, which depressed Harrison's spirits more than they were already depressed. All in all, Sister Constance's orphanage was a stark contrast to the warmth and happiness of Mr. Siddel's establishment.

"Here you are, my lords." Sister Constance stopped just inside of a mid-sized chapel at the end of the long hallway. It looked as though the chapel were a much earlier structure than the rest of the building, as if the orphanage had been tacked onto a centuries-old church. "You are more than welcome to search for your ring here."

"Thank you, sister," John said with a solemn bow. As

soon as Sister Constance left them to their search, John cracked into a grin. "Can you imagine the sort of life a child would have in a place like this?"

"At least the ones we saw looked well-fed and warm," Harrison replied with a sigh, glancing around.

The chapel was as much of a jumble as Sister Constance implied it would be. Several of the pews at the back of the room were stacked with crates and baskets of donations that looked like those that had been given at the hall in Clerkenwell. But there were other boxes and sacks of things piled at the front of the room. In addition to that, several movable racks of clothing lined the edges of the room where various alcoves for stations of the cross stood. Beyond that, there were building supplies in one corner of the room, and a rather rickety scaffolding appeared to be holding up a section of the roof.

"Well, I suppose the only way to find the ring is to start looking," Harrison said with a sigh.

They headed to the first row of pews holding donations and started their search. As impressed as Harrison was with the generosity of those who had given to Bianca's cause, shifting through crates of books and old clothes left him with even more of a sense of urgency.

"I don't know what I'll do if I can't find it," he said, half to himself.

"You'll do what you have to do," John told him from the pew across the aisle as he searched himself. "You'll do what any man docs when they find themselves in a particular situation like this."

Harrison glanced up from the basket he was rifling through to find John grinning at him like a fool. He matched that grin with a wry look of his own. "And I suppose you would do the same thing if you found yourself in a similar position?"

"Ah," John replied. "But I would never find myself in that position, because I would never be so silly as to find myself in love."

A small thump sounded from the corner of the room near the door. Harrison glanced casually in that direction, but the doorway was empty. All he saw was one of the racks of clothing and a pile of crates that were stacked nearly to the ceiling beside it. For the briefest of moments he thought that he saw a flicker of movement, but he chalked it up to the draft that ran through the building blowing some of the hanging clothes.

"Come off it," he continued, shaking his head at John as he moved on to the next pew and the items it contained. "You're even more in love than I am, if such a thing is possible."

"Ha!" John barked, stepping into his next pew as well. "No one could possibly be as deeply in love as you are."

"Oh, no?" It was Harrison's turn to laugh. "Spare me. You've been dancing around Diana since Reese's house party last year."

"Dancing around someone is not the same as being madly in love with them," John said. He abandoned the crates in his pew and strode up to the front of the chapel to see what was waiting there.

Harrison sorted through a basket at the end of his pew, and when he found nothing, he gave up with a sigh and move up the aisle to join John near the chancel. "You can pretend all you like, but you and Diana flirt shamelessly at every opportunity."

"That's not flirting," John chuckled. "If I was going to flirt with Diana, you would know it."

Out of the corner of his eye, Harrison thought he spotted another bit of movement. But when he turned to the side aisle, once again, he saw nothing but the clutter that packed the alcoves. He might have heard something that sounded like whispering, but as likely as not, it was mice. Churches were full of them, after all.

"If what you and Diana are engaged in isn't a flirtation of the highest order," he went on, turning his attention back to the work at hand, "then I don't know what flirtation is."

"You said it, not me," John laughed.

"Ah, but I most certainly do know what flirtation is," Harrison went on, a bit wistfully. "I only wish there were more I could do with Bea at the moment than flirt with her."

"Nothing is stopping you from making your grand declaration—oh! Is this it?"

Harrison abandoned the sack of old shoes he was searching through to join John on the other side of the aisle. Again, he could have sworn he heard a thump or clatter of some sort, but when he looked over his shoulder, nothing was there.

He turned his attention to the box of sundries John had uncovered in an old suitcase that had been left at the edge of the pew. It contained several ring boxes, but it was clear at a glance that none of them were the one containing his great-grandmother's ring.

"What on earth is this?" he asked, leaning closer to John as he reached for a bright red velvet ring box. He opened it, only to find it was empty.

"Can you imagine the monstrosity this must have contained?" John asked. "Red velvet." He snorted. "I mean, really." He took the box from Harrison and leaned in closer. "Only a bit or bauble given by a man to his mistress should be housed in red velvet."

Harrison cleared his throat, his face heating. They were in a bloody church. They shouldn't have been discussing things like mistresses or gifting them with gems mere yards away from the Holy Bible. Because of that, he hunched closer to John, almost as though the two of them were engaged in some sort of conspiracy, and whispered, "Not in church, John. Besides, I thought you looked down on men who kept mistresses."

"I do," John said, playing along and whispering as though they were naughty schoolboys. "But I also recognize that these things happen."

A creak sounded from the opposite end of the room that had Harrison flinching back, as though they'd been caught. He couldn't shake the feeling that they were being watched, but when he glanced around, the chapel was exactly as it had been before. The only thing he could figure had caused the creak was the scaffolding supporting the section of the roof.

"Do you suppose this is safe?" he asked, stepping away from John and moving to examine the structure.

"It looks sound enough." John followed him.

Harrison stared up at the ceiling, then went so far as to climb a few rungs of the scaffolding to make certain the whole thing was in good shape. As far as he could see, there was a door of some sort in the ceiling that was tightly closed. He figured it had been used at some point in the church's history to climb out onto the roof in order to clean or chase away birds. Perhaps there had even been a belfry on the other side. Either way, the trapdoor was securely fastened with a latch.

"It looks fine," he said as he climbed back down the scaffold to resume his search. John followed him back to the pew with the collection of ring boxes. "Nothing out of the ordinary. I wonder if the scaffolding is there because they plan to seal the door."

"Who knows?" John shrugged and the two of them got back to work.

A few minutes later, Burt skittered into the chapel, glancing over his shoulder as if someone were chasing him.

"And what are you up to, lad?" John asked with a grin.

Burt stopped so suddenly that he nearly fell over. "I

didn't see you in here, my lord," he said, his face going pink.

"Well, as long as you're here, why don't you make yourself useful and help us search," John said.

"Um." Burt jerked this way and that, either looking for whoever he thought was chasing him or for an excuse to get out of doing work. His eyes alighted on the scaffolding in the corner, and his expression flickered to a grin. "All right, my lord. If you insist."

"I do," John said.

Burt ambled his way up the center aisle, hands in his pockets—which seemed to be filled with something, though Harrison could only imagine what it was—until he reached the chancel. "Maybe it fell up here," he said, climbing up a few steps and turning in a circle as he looked up at the ceiling.

Harrison ignored the boy. He had always been eager to get out of work whenever possible at that age himself. But at the moment, he was highly motivated to do the work in front of him.

Only, within a few more moments, it was clear that the ring wasn't there.

He straightened, huffing a sigh. "If only—"

His words were cut off by a clatter near the chancel. He and John both whipped around to see what it was, but again, eerily, it was nothing. Burt, too, looked startled from where he was perched halfway up the scaffold.

Harrison cleared his throat and turned to John. "If

only I had gone straight home after visiting Grandmama the other day. I could have avoided this whole thing."

"You were eager to help out with the cause," John said, shrugging and giving up his own search. "And, I suspect, you were eager to see your sweetheart again."

"I probably was." Harrison let out a breath and pushed a hand through his hair. "That's the last time I do something impulsive. It's not worth the risk. I should have known better."

"Everything will work out for the best," John said, thumping his back and starting up the aisle to the back of the chapel. "You'll see." They made it halfway to the back of the church before John glanced over his shoulder and called, "Burt, are you coming?"

"Yes, my lord. Right away, my lord." Burt scrambled down from the scaffolding and dashed down the aisle to join Harrison and John, all arms and legs.

"What were you doing up there anyhow?" John asked as they exited the chapel.

"Getting a better view, my lord," Burt said, mischief in his eyes. "Ain't that what they always say to do? When you can't figure something out up close, take a step back and get a better view?"

"You're absolutely right," John said, thumping Burt's back. "You hear that, Harrison? We have a philosopher here. If things seem bleak up close, take a step back and reassess the situation."

Harrison laughed and shook his head, though he didn't see how stepping back from a missing ring and his undying love for Bea was going to help anything. What he needed to do next was face the problem head-on and propose like he should have all along, whether it was the stuff the poets wrote about or not. Otherwise, he ran the risk of letting Bea, and his life, get away from him.

CHAPTER 7

"Ow!" Bea let out the exclamation as Diana trampled on the hem of her dress, then immediately stifled her outburst with a hand to her mouth.

She and Diana were hunkered behind a rack of old clothes in various states of repair, concealed from view— she hoped—from Harrison and John. The men had yet to notice they'd snuck into the chapel as they picked through the donations. They'd reached the first pew at the front of the room. Bea couldn't imagine what they were looking for. They didn't appear to be sorting the donations. From the moment she and Diana had crept into the room, all they seemed to be doing was looking through them, as though they were vegetables at market and the two were deciding what they wanted to have for supper that night.

"Ssh." Diana silenced Bea with a wave of her hand,

79

then swayed toward the clothing hanging in front of them. With all of the grace of a burglar, Diana parted the coats, shirts, and bodices to peer out through the donated clothing at the men. "They're up to something, I just know it."

Bea rocked back, sitting on the edge of the stone outcropping that made up part of the alcove behind the rack. "While I will agree that their behavior is suspicious," she whispered, "I hardly think they're up to no good."

"It's John," Diana murmured over her shoulder. "That man is always trouble."

Bea pressed her lips together and stared at Diana's back. She loved her friend like a sister, but Diana most certainly had a blind spot where John was concerned. If she would just loosen up her tight hold of her pride and admit she had feelings for the man, her misery could be resolved.

Then again, knowing and admitting that she was in love with Harrison hadn't done Bea a lick of good. Not when she had made a fool out of herself for his sake, and not when she was reasonably certain she stood on the precipice of making a fool of herself again that very moment. She and Diana were poor spies, and Bea was convinced the men would realize they were there at any second.

Movement near the door to the chapel caught her eye, and Bea turned slightly to see Burt dash into the room.

"And what are you up to, lad?" Bea heard John ask.

"I didn't see you in here, my lord," Burt answered.

Bea stood and crept over to the rack of clothes through which Diana was spying.

"Well, as long as you're here, why don't you make yourself useful and help us search," John said.

Burt moved forward, though with her limited range of vision behind the curtain of coats, Bea could only assume he went to the chancel instead of actually seeing him.

"So they are searching for something," she whispered to Diana.

"He's searching for his soul, if he knows what's good for him," Diana growled.

Bea sent her friend a flat look and leaned back. She hooked her hand in the crook of Diana's arm, pulling her away from her spying as she went. Diana looked livid at being interrupted, but kept her mouth shut. Then again, she didn't need to speak. Bea could tell just how frustrated she was by the fury in her eyes.

"Diana, really," Bea whispered, sending a quick glance in the direction of the men, even though they were blocked from view. "This vendetta with John has become childish."

"He is the one who is childish," Diana hissed in return, stepping close to Bea so that they could remain as quiet as possible. "Only a man-child would play pranks on unsuspecting orphanages at Christmastime."

Bea let out a breath and fought not to roll her eyes.

"Are you certain that this fixation with John as a prankster isn't because you, like me, are desperate for a proposal that has been painfully slow in coming?"

Diana squeaked in indignation, then clamped her jaw hard and pressed a hand to her mouth. She sent a furious glance in the direction of the men—one that was so sharp it could have cut right through the donated clothes—before glaring at Bea. "I wouldn't marry John Darrow if he were the last man on earth. Why, he's arrogant and devilish and...and arrogant, and I would never—"

A change in the men's conversation stopped Diana in the middle of her rant. She and Bea rushed back to the rack, doing their best to stay hidden while watching Harrison and John walk up the aisle and out of the chapel. Burt left with them.

Bea and Diana stayed where they were, bodies tense, holding their breaths, until the sound of the men's footsteps and their conversation faded into nothing. Once they were well and truly gone, Bea stepped out from behind the clothes and walked toward the front row of pews. She heaved a sigh as she sank into the pew.

"I should face the fact that he's never going to propose," she said. "Clearly, he has far too many important things occupying his mind to bother marrying me."

"Now who's being childish," Diana said, marching up to her and crossing her arms.

"I am being the opposite of childish," Bea said, sitting

straighter. "I am facing the truth of a situation that, I fear, I had built up in my mind to be something other than what it is."

"Nonsense." Diana sat in the pew beside her. Bea expected her to launch into a tirade of some sort, but instead, she let out a heavy breath, her shoulders sinking. "This is what comes of not allowing women to have any sort of profession or interests outside of the domestic sphere," she said, picking at a spot of dirt on her skirt. "Without any sort of serious purpose, we're left with nothing to occupy our minds but fantasies and fussing."

Bea cracked into a wry grin. "We're relegated to this, and then men turn around and say that our minds are not fit for any sort of seriousness or employment."

Diana let out a sullen laugh. "They have created the very situation they revile us for."

"I don't want to be a ninny," Bea said, with all due seriousness. "I'm sure there are a thousand more productive things I could apply my mind to besides worrying whether Harrison will propose or not."

"And my intellectual capabilities are much better suited toward steering this country and our world in a progressive direction than they are toward worrying whether some silly man is playing pranks on orphans," Diana agreed. "Which is precisely why it is so important that the May Flowers takes a stand for the rights of women." She stood, as if to prove her point, and Bea stood with her. "That is why, as soon as this Christmas event is over, I am going to take a stand, once and for all, and ally the May Flowers with any and all of the new organizations supporting the rights of women that have been forming of late."

"Hear, hear," Bea said, cheering her on.

"I will begin those efforts as soon as I figure out what John was up to by meddling with these donations." Diana turned and started picking her way through the boxes and baskets lining the front pew.

Bea sighed, tempted to laugh. They had come so close to putting their minds and effort toward something noble. But old habits died hard. She glanced toward the chapel's door, half wishing Harrison would waltz back through with his arms outstretched and a proposal on his lips.

That thought had her laughing at herself as she followed Diana across the front of the chapel. It was one thing to be high-minded, but love had plans of its own, especially when one had a heart that felt purpose-built to love.

She was on the verge of telling Diana that they didn't truly have a way to discover what the men had been looking for and to give up her efforts so that they could return to Clerkenwell when she spotted a thick string dangling down from the ceiling in the middle of the scaffolding in the corner of the chapel. Perplexed, she stepped closer to get a good look. She hadn't given the scaffolding much thought when they'd entered the room. Wondering what Harrison was doing had most of her attention then. She couldn't recall if the string had been there before. There was something intriguing about the way it was tied, though. It was somehow fastened to the ceiling, though she couldn't quite tell how. The end was close enough for her to reach. She grabbed it, and fueled by the sort of undeniable curiosity that killed cats, she pulled.

Something clicked above her, and in a flash, a wide trapdoor opened, and a cascade of brown, foul-smelling, ice-cold water splashed down on her.

Bea screamed as the dirty water instantly soaked her from head to toe, chilling her to the bone.

"Dear God!" Diana shouted, rushing toward her and pulling Bea out of the way of the stream of filth that continued to rain down. "Help! Help!" she called.

Once she was out of the direct assault of the water, details began to fall into place. Not only was the water filthy, it was mixed with dead leaves, sticks, and even bits of old newspapers. Chances were that it was run-off from gutters around the church's roof. Whatever it was, Bea let out a miserable yelp and shook her arms as if she could brush the refuse away.

"I knew it," Diana growled, pulling Bea toward the aisle as Sister Constance and a handful of young nuns dashed into the room. "I knew that they were up to no good."

"Mercy's sake, what is going on in here?" Sister Constance boomed as she dashed up the aisle.

"Those so-called gentlemen that you let invade your

establishment have pulled the most horrid prank," Diana answered, leaping to the side to grab a donated shirt from one of the racks of clothes. She used it to swab Bea's face, though Bea felt rather like she was being battered in the process. "They rigged the ceiling to collapse," Diana went on.

"Oh, dear," one of the nuns said as she came to a stop at the bottom of the scaffolding. "I knew we should have prioritized fixing the drains."

"We can barely afford to feed the children," one of the others said as she, too, examined the mess around the scaffolding. "I'm surprised it didn't leak long before this."

"It did," the first nun said. "That's what Sister Francine was trying to fix this morning."

"She wouldn't have caused this, though, would she?"

"It wasn't Sister Francine, it was Lord Whitlock," Diana insisted in a rage. "He and his accomplice were meddling with the scaffolding, and who knows what else in the room, just moments before Bea was doused. In fact, stand back." She held out her arms, glaring suspiciously at the donations around her. "They could have planted any number of traps in the rest of these things."

"What sort of nonsense are you on about, my lady?" Sister Constance said, frowning at Diana as though she were another of her orphans.

"Don't you see?" Diana stepped closer to her. "It all makes sense. Lord Whitlock and Lord Landsbury are the pranksters that have been menacing several orphanages in the last few days."

"My lady." Sister Constance fixed Diana with a scolding look. "Why in heaven's name would two noblemen, one of them a viscount, for Christ's sake, stoop so low as to cause mischief in orphanages."

Bea's eyes snapped wide at the nun's bit of blasphemy before her mouth twitched into a grin. There was no telling who or what Sister Constance had been before taking her vows.

The wild thought gave her the courage to stand up to Diana and say, "I think Sister Constance it right. Pranks might not be beneath Harrison and John in our circles, but they would never resort to teasing orphans."

"Quite right, my lady." Sister Constance nodded in approval.

"But John and Harrison were present at each of the orphanages that were pranked," Diana said, tilting her chin up as though offended no one believed her. "They were just at Mr. Siddel's orphanage when that box of ferrets was let loose—"

"A box of ferrets?" one of the nuns asked in horror.

"Dozens of them," Bea said.

"—and they were at Hope Orphanage yesterday," Diana went on.

"Were they at St. Joseph's the day before that?" Bea asked, wadding the damp shirt she'd used to clean her face into a ball and wondering if she could use it to clean her coat. It was likely that the unfortunate garment was ruined.

"I would be willing to wager they were," Diana said.

"Here, my lady." Sister Constance stepped forward, hands outstretched. "Let me take that spoiled thing off of you. Sisters Katherine and Angelica will take you somewhere you can wash your face and hair. And we can lend you something to keep you warm on your journey home."

"Thank you," Bea said, as gracious as she could be as the nun helped her to remove her coat. At the last minute, she remembered the parcel Annie from Mr. Siddel's orphanage had given her and reached into the pocket to retrieve it. "I'm afraid that poor thing is ruined," she sighed as she turned the parcel over and over in her hands. "It will probably need to be burned."

"Nonsense," Sister Constance said, handing the coat to one of the nuns. "We'll get the stink out and return it to you."

"Or you could sell it," Bea suggested. "Consider it my donation to your establishment."

The nun who received Bea's coat brightened at the prospect and turned to carry the offensive garment away.

"Yes, this is all well and good," Diana said impatiently. "But we need to plot a way to expose John and Harrison for the blackguards they are."

Sister Constance pursed her lips and sent Diana a flat look.

Bea was busy trying to figure out if the package she was supposed to return to Harrison would fit in any of the pockets of her skirts. "Diana, you need to move on to greener pastures. The gents didn't do this." She sucked in a breath as a thought hit her. "It was probably that little scamp, Burt. He was at each of the orphanages where pranks were pulled as well."

"If he was, it was only because he was in John's employ," Diana said. A slow grin spread across her face. "But I know just the thing to expose the villain once and for all."

Bea was filled with a feeling of dread that went ten times deeper than anything she'd felt when the icy gutter water splashed down on her. "Oh, dear," she sighed, sending Sister Constance a long-suffering look.

"I'll catch him out at the party tomorrow night," Diana went on, a devious light in her eyes. "I'll force him to confess in front of everyone just what kind of nuisance he is. That'll show him."

"This is precisely why I took orders," Sister Constance said, rolling her eyes. "Men and love are far too much trouble."

"I am not in love with John Darrow," Diana said through clenched teeth.

"Of course, you aren't, dearie," Sister Constance said, patting Diana's shoulders while sending Bea a sardonic look.

It was all Bea could do not to laugh, in spite of the cold and the smell surrounding her. Diana was as in love as she was.

Which gave her an idea. If Diana was determined to call John out for pranks—that Bea was certain he hadn't pulled—at the party, then perhaps she could bring things to a head with Harrison as far as marriage was concerned. After all, Bianca had encouraged her to take things into her own hands. Seduction was one way to do that, but there were dozens of others she could try.

# CHAPTER 8

The simple hall in Clerkenwell had undergone a complete transformation by the time Harrison arrived for the party on Christmas Eve. Its drab walls were hung with garlands of holly and pine accentuated by bright red bows and silver bells. More garlands had been strung from the rafters and decorated with paper snowflakes made by the orphans of the various institutions that the party was intended to support. The effect was almost as if they were in a snowy forest. Several Christmas trees had been brought in and decorated with shiny baubles of all descriptions. Some of the older boys stood guard over the trees, minding the candles that illuminated their boughs.

Dozens upon dozens of wrapped gifts were nestled under the trees, and already boys and girls of all ages were crowding around to gaze at them in wonder. A few of the bolder children even picked up the gifts to shake them, as though they could guess what was inside. They were minded by women, and a few men, as in the case of Stephen Siddel—who had as many youngsters crowded around him and gazing at him in awe as if he were Father Christmas himself—taking care that no serious harm came to the gifts. Each of them was decked out in what Harrison was certain were their very best clothes, though the circles of society that he ran in would likely say they looked shabby. They would have been wrong. Everyone in the hall appeared happy, and happiness was the most attractive garment of all.

Tables stretched along one wall containing refreshments of all sorts. Harrison recognized several members of the May Flowers, friends of his, manning the treats, including Henrietta O'Shea and Cecelia Marlowe. They were some of the highest-ranking women in the room, and yet they blended in with the middle- and working-class women as though they had all gone to school together.

It was as cheery a sight as Harrison could imagine and a testament to Bianca's organizational skills, but Harrison's heart was heavy for so many reasons, not least of which was the woman on his arm. His beloved grandmother had insisted on attending the party with him. By the looks of her, she was enjoying herself immensely, even though it was necessary for her to use a cane to get around in her old age. Harrison scanned the room for a chair where she could sit, but even as he spotted one, he had the feeling she wouldn't be relegated to the corners of the room quietly.

"Where is that fetching sweetheart of yours?" she asked as Harrison steered her over to the Christmas trees so that she could watch the bright-faced and excited children. "I was given to believe she would be at this party."

Harrison sent her a wary, sideways look. "I'm certain she'll be here at any moment, Grandmama. She and Lady Diana were instrumental in carrying this whole thing off."

His grandmother hummed and glanced up at him with a knowing smile. "I expect to see the darling creature wearing my ring when she arrives."

Self-consciousness slithered down Harrison's spine. "Yes, well, there may be a slight problem with that."

His grandmother looked surprised. "You have proposed to her by now, haven't you?"

"I intended to propose this evening," he said, tugging at his collar. The room suddenly seemed entirely too warm with too many people crowding around.

"Intended to?" His grandmother looked shocked. "You mean you didn't run straight to that angel's house to drop down on one knee the moment I handed over Mother's ring?"

Sweat began to creep down Harrison's back. "Yes, well, you see, there was a slight hiccup with the whole process."

He cleared his throat, rolled his shoulders, and scrambled for a way to confess he'd lost the family ring. More than that, he feared he would have to confess that it was gone forever. He and John hadn't spotted so much as a glint of it, and they'd checked every box at every orphanage the donations had been taken to. The only explanation he could think of was that someone had discovered the ring and lifted it for their own financial gain. For all he knew, some middle-class housewife was about to unwrap the most precious Christmas present of her life, thanks to his carelessness. And now he had to confess all to his grandmother.

He opened his mouth, praying that he'd find the right words to make himself look foolish without appearing criminally stupid, but every thought blasted out of his head as he spotted Bea in the doorway. She was simply the most beautiful thing he'd ever seen, so much so that the breath left his lungs. She wore a magnificent gown of festive red and had her red-gold hair caught up in the latest style, a glittering pin holding it in place. The cut of her gown showed off her shapely figure, and the expanse of skin it exposed across her chest and shoulders was as pure as porcelain. The blush that kissed her face was the stuff artists would have scrambled over each other to paint, and the hope in her eyes as she searched the room left him ready to leap into action or fall at her feet if she wanted him to.

As if she could hear his thoughts and feel the force of

his love, she glanced right at him and smiled. If Harrison had trouble breathing before, that trouble was tenfold when he saw the way her eyes glittered, even across the room, as they met his.

His grandmother huffed a laugh at his side. "Well, my boy," she said, grinning from ear to ear. "You'd better stop dragging your feet and propose to that fine lady before one of the other gentlemen in this hall sees her and snatches her up."

"Would that I could," Harrison sighed before he could check himself.

His grandmother turned to him. "And just what is that supposed to mean?"

"I...um...."

Harrison was spared having to come up with an excuse, or confessing about losing her ring, when John strode up to him and clapped him on the back. "This isn't fair at all," he said with a rakish look for Grandmama. "How is it that this miscreant has snagged the finest lady in the room this evening?"

"Good evening yourself, Lord Whitlock," Harrison's grandmother said, sending John a look that said she was too old and had seen too much to fall for his tricks. She did, however, let go of Harrison's arm so that she could tuck her hand into the crook of John's elbow. "You always were a rascal," she said with a chuckle.

"A rascal with excellent taste in women, Lady Landsbury," John said, leaning over to give Harrison's grandmother a kiss. "Has this one been telling you all about the mischief we've been getting into?"

Harrison was only half paying attention to the exchange. He'd been watching Bea as she entered the room fully, greeting Bianca and Jack, who stood by the door, looking like Clerkenwell royalty. Bea was the personification of grace and cheer as she embraced Bianca and let Jack kiss her hand. She was considerate enough to turn to her father and sister—who Harrison only just noticed had accompanied her—as if making a formal introduction, though Harrison was certain they'd met before. He even spotted Diana arriving a moment behind Bea before John's question dragged him back to the conversation right next to him.

"No," Grandmama answered with a smirk. "My dear grandson has been close-lipped about everything he's been up to since calling on me for a particular purpose earlier this week." She arched an eyebrow for John, who met it with a conspiratorial look of his own. "You wouldn't know why he has kept so silent, would you?"

"There's nothing to report," Harrison said with a nervous laugh, sending John a look that practically begged him to keep his mouth shut.

A contradiction of a different sort reared its head before Harrison could finish his defense. Lord Lichfield, Bea's father, broke away from Bianca and Jack and his daughters, catching Harrison's eye and marching straight across the increasingly crowded and noisy hall toward him. Harrison sucked in a breath and snapped as straight as he could, reminding himself that he was a marquess, he loved Bea and had every intention of asking for her hand as soon as possible, and that he and Lord Lichfield really did have the same aim.

"Good evening, Lady Landsbury." Lord Lichfield greeted Harrison's grandmother first, giving Harrison what he hoped were a few more moments of reprieve. "What a delight to see you at such a festive occasion this evening."

"It was far more appealing to me than sitting through yet another long, dry Christmas Eve sermon, Lord Lichfield," Grandmama said with a grin.

Harrison laughed—perhaps a little too loudly—at his grandmother's quip. Fortunately, Lord Lichfield laughed as well. Their two families had been friends dating back to the Regency, when Harrison's great-grandmother and Lord Lichfield's grandmother had caused all sorts of mischief together after being blacklisted by the *ton* and shunned by polite society. The ladies and their friends, including John's great-grandmother, had made their own society, as well as causing more than a few scandals.

Harrison grasped onto the hope that Lord Lichfield and his grandmother would say something about their family connections, but his hopes were dashed when Lord Lichfield turned a frown on him and said, "I was rather hoping you would come to see me, as I insisted you should, before this evening, young man."

Harrison gulped, panic seeping around the edges of his gentlemanly calm. "These last few days have been mad-capped, my lord," he said by way of an excuse.

"I was rather hoping my grandson had come to see you about something much sooner, my lord," Grandmama said, her mischievous old eyes twinkling. "Preferably last summer, but after I spoke with him on Monday at the latest."

Lord Lichfield's brow lifted, and he and Grandmama grinned at each other. "It seems as though you and I are of the same mind on a certain subject," he said. Both of them turned to study Harrison. "Particularly after I caught your grandson in a tender embrace with my Beatrice the other evening."

"Harrison, you scoundrel," Grandmama said with mock horror. There was enough of a flash in her eyes to suggest to Harrison that she herself had been caught in far more scandalous situations than the kiss Harrison and Bea had shared in Lord Lichfield's dining room. "This is why young people these days should not be left up to their own devices," she went on with a chuckle.

"I may have to agree with you on that one, Lady Landsbury," Diana said, charging up to join their group without greeting or preamble, fury etched in the lines of her handsome face.

Harrison knew he needed to say something to stave off whatever attack Diana was clearly about to hurl at John, but he was bowled over by the anxiety painting Bea's face as she rushed up to her friend.

"Oh, Diana, don't. Please," Bea whispered.

Harrison could only imagine what was about to happen. Instinct took over, and he immediately shifted to Bea's side, reaching for her hand as if the battle were about to begin.

"Lady Diana," John said with cheeky calm, raking her from head to toe. Clearly, he appreciated what he saw, as would anyone with eyes. Diana was dressed in a stunning and fashionable gown of deep blue that made her dramatic features even more stunning. John, being John, let his gaze linger at her décolletage, likely in a gesture designed to antagonize Diana even more.

"You cannot hide the truth from me for a moment longer, John," Diana said, shaking a finger at him. "I know what you have been up to, you and your nefarious accomplice." She spared a quick glance for Harrison, but it was obvious to all who the subject of her anger was. "You have been found out at last, and you will pay for your mischief."

"I would gladly pay, sweet Diana," John said with unflappable calm, even though the rest of them were struck with one degree of shock or another. "As long as you are meting out punishment." He finished with a saucy wink that had Harrison's grandmother snorting with laughter.

Diana pulled herself up to her full height. "The nerve of you," she hissed.

"Diana," Bea said in a soothing voice, resting a hand on her friend's arm. "Perhaps now is not the time to—"

"Tart?"

The interruption came from none other than Burt, who was clean and groomed and holding out a tray of savory tarts, his grin fixed on Diana. The boy was so cheeky that Harrison almost laughed.

"I love a good tart myself," John said without missing a beat. He plucked a bite-sized morsel from Burt's tray and bit into it, staring at Diana all the while.

"You are impossible," Diana huffed. "Pretending to be innocent when everyone knows that you are the miscreant who has been pulling pranks on London's orphanages."

Of all things, Burt looked mortally offended by Diana's assertion.

"Whatever makes you think I would be capable of such a thing?" John laughed, then finished off his tart.

"Deeds like that are precisely the sort of thing a wretch like you would get up to," Diana said, tilting her chin up and refusing to look at him. Except for when she peeked at him as if hoping he could continue their sparring match.

"Some toff shouldn't get all the credit for ingenuity," Burt said, slinking away with a scowl. He continued to mutter, but Harrison had more pressing things to give his attention to than the hurt feelings of a working-class lad.

"Confess your crimes, John, or I will make them known to everyone at this party," Diana went on.

"Really, Diana," Bea whispered. "Now is not the time—"

"Go right ahead," John said, forced to raise his voice somewhat as the band Bianca had hired to play for the party burst into a lively waltz. "But before you do, dance with me."

"I would never—oh!" Diana attempted to protest, but John swept his arm around her and led her to the center of the hall as party guests cleared to make way for dancing.

"My grandson isn't the only one who needs to hurry up and propose," Harrison's grandmother muttered to Lord Lichfield.

"Indeed," Lord Lichfield agreed as the two of them grinned and shook their heads at John and Diana.

Harrison turned to Bea, expecting her to look mortified because of their friends' behavior, but instead, her eyes were as wide as saucers as she stared at him. "Are you really going to—"

"Ask you to dance?" Harrison cut her off, holding out a hand to her as his face heated. "Of course."

"Oh." Bea blinked, then took Harrison's hand and allowed him to lead her out to the center of the floor.

Harrison didn't know why he'd cut Bea off, only that he wanted whatever proposal he made to be perfect. Not that there was any chance of that now. The ring was gone, his grandmother had tipped his cards, hinting to Bea that the proposal was coming, and even if he hadn't had plans to proceed on his own timetable, Lord Lichfield was determined to see things through for him. It was as far from the romantic moment Harrison had dreamed of, the moment Bea deserved, than he could have imagined. The whole thing was turning out to be a source of stress instead of joy. But it was all water under the bridge now. He might as well go ahead and ask the question that needed to be asked.

"Bea, would you—"

"Did you and John plot—"

They spoke at the same time. They each stopped speaking at the same time and blinked at each other as well, even stumbling through the waltz steps, like two children just learning the simple dance, as they did.

"I'm sorry, you—"

"I beg your pard—"

Again, they spoke over each other, and nearly stepped on each other's feet as they did.

"You first—"

"After you—"

The third time, they both broke into laughter. Bea's face turned the most charming shade of pink. Coupled with her red dress and her golden hair, it made her look as warm and inviting as a flame. He would forever be the moth that sought to get closer to her.

"I have tried so hard to make everything perfect for you," Harrison said, letting out a breath and pulling her deeper into his arms as they danced. "You deserve everything and then some."

"I don't truly need *everything*," Bea said, her face tilted down just enough that when she glanced up at him through her lashes, it caused Harrison's heart to skip a beat. Something expectant remained in her gaze as she watched him, waiting for the conversation to go on.

"Bea, I—"

He didn't have the chance to say what he wanted to say before John and Diana nearly rammed into them from the side. John looked as though he were having the time of his life as he led Diana through a few more complicated waltz steps. Diana looked as though she were trying to wrestle the lead from him. Neither said a word, but then again, words weren't needed to communicate what the two of them were saying to each other.

"They are impossible," Bea sighed, shaking her head.

"Something must be done," Harrison agreed. "But later. For now...." He paused, maneuvering Bea through a few waltz steps and whirling her toward the edge of the dancers. He wanted to keep her in his arms as long as possible while having as much privacy as they could muster in the crowded hall. "Bea, I can't hold my feelings for you inside any longer. I've tried so hard these last few days to make things perfect. I even spoke to Grandmama, and she gave me a ring that once belonged to her mother for the purpose I had in mind. But then everything went pear-shaped. I lost the ring."

"Oh." Bea's expression lit up, as though she'd figured out the solution to a puzzle.

"And I got caught up in preparations for this party," he went on. "And what with your father the other evening...." Harrison sighed. "What I am trying to say is—"

Before he could finish, the party came to a sudden and explosive halt, quite literally, as a flurry of fire-crackers exploded in the center of the room.

## CHAPTER 9

One moment Bea was waltzing away in a cloud of happiness, overjoyed to be in Harrison's arms at last. In a way that didn't cause her father to scold or tease her. The evening was turning out to be far more wonderful than she would have imagined a party for orphans could have been. And above all, she had the excited feeling that maybe, just maybe, Harrison intended to propose at last.

The next moment the hall was in utter chaos. Sharp cracks and the acrid scent of gunpowder filled the air, along with the screams of women and children. The band stopped playing, and the couples that had been dancing away with varying degrees of bliss dove for the edges of the room.

"We're under attack!" a traumatized, male voice called from one corner of the room. "Call the militia!"

Bea caught a flurry of movement out of the corner of

her eye as several women rushed toward a relatively young man who had hunkered in on himself at the first, startling cracks. "He's a war veteran," one of them shouted in a furious tone as she threw her arms around him. "You're all right, Billy."

The initial burst of sharp, staccato explosions was followed by another before Bea realized that the noise wasn't being caused by gunfire, but rather by a string of cheap firecrackers that had been lit and tossed into the center of the dancing couples. That didn't stop her heart from racing as the fireworks exhausted themselves, leaving a puff of foul-smelling smoke in their wake.

The couples who had darted to the sides of the room recovered slowly. Bea noticed one middle-class woman beating at her skirt, which bore a sad, burned mark. She was the only one who seemed to have been damaged by the prank. A few women were crying, and a few men raised shaking hands to wipe sweat away from their brows, leaving Bea to think poor Billy wasn't the only traumatized war veteran in the room.

What Bea found particularly interesting, though, was the way Diana trembled in John's arms. They had retreated to the side of the room, like all of the other couples, and Diana had her face hidden against John's shoulder. His arms were firmly around her, his expression serious, and if Bea wasn't mistaken, he was whispering soothing words into her ear, as though the sole focus of his world was to make her feel safe and secure.

The way Diana clung to him told Bea that John's efforts were working.

Bea grinned over the picture her friends painted before stopping to consider that she was tucked in Harrison's arms in a similar pose of protectiveness.

"Are you all right?" Harrison asked, rubbing a soothing hand across her back.

"I am," Bea said, straightening and sucking in a breath. "But what a fright."

There was one person in the room who wasn't the least bit shaken by the explosive prank. Not only wasn't he shaken, Burt was nearly doubled over in laughter, pointing at some of the more frightened ladies as they wept into their handkerchiefs. "Look at the lot of you," he laughed. "Crying over a couple of crackers."

Bea gaped at the lad, astounded that he could be laughing over such a cruel-minded prank, but even more when Jack Craig marched toward him, looking as though Hell were on his heels.

"That's enough from you, boy," Jack said, grabbing Burt by his collar and glaring at him.

Whatever other faults Burt had, he had the good sense to look duly terrified as he was forced to face Jack. "It was just a joke, sir, just a joke," he insisted, the color draining from his face.

"Crackers are not a joke," Jack growled, shaking Burt, and then letting him go. "People could have been hurt."

"Not by those little things," Burt said, lowering his

head and hunching his shoulders. "They were the small ones."

"What on earth possessed you to do something so idiotic in the middle of a Christmas party?" Jack asked on, standing tall and crossing his arms.

Burt got some of his cockiness back. "They were trying to take credit for all I did." He flung an arm out toward John, pointing and glaring. "I put a lot of work into those pranks, and I won't have some nob saying he did it."

"You were the scamp who poured treacle on the books at St. Joseph's?" one of the women who had been involved in the conversation days ago said, her expression one of shock and outrage.

"You replaced all of our sugar with salt?" a woman Bea recognized as the matron of Hope Orphanage said, glaring at Burt.

"How in God's name did you smuggle a box with two dozen ferrets into my orphanage?" Stephen Siddel asked, though, Bea noted, with a spark in his eyes that said he was impressed. "Where did you even get two dozen ferrets?"

"My cousin, Bob, catches 'em in nobs' gardens and disposes of them," Burt said with a proud look. "Only, he's been keeping them as pets. We were bringing boxes from here into the orphanage anyhow, and no one noticed what I had in the box."

Bea tilted her head to the side, reluctantly impressed as well. At least, until she remembered the scent of the filthy water that had doused her at the Sisters of Perpetual Sorrow the day before. "You rigged the trap door in Sister Constance's chapel to spill filth all over me, didn't you?" She narrowed her eyes at the boy.

Harrison flinched. "You were in the Sisters of Perpetual Sorrows' chapel?"

Bea didn't have time to answer before Burt turned to her, wringing his hands. "That was supposed to be for the nuns. Sorry, my lady. You're awful nice, and I didn't want to do it to you like that." The audacious lad actually made eyes at Bea, as though he had boyish feelings for her. That image was shattered a moment later when he went on to say, "You should have seen the look on your face," and started laughing again.

Jack put a swift end to the laughter. "That's enough out of you, Burt. You're just lucky nothing you did is a criminal offense. That won't stop me from having a word with the headmaster of your orphanage, though." He grabbed Burt's arm and marched him toward the door.

"I swear, I won't do anything like that again," Burt scrambled to say. "I'll be a perfect angel from now on, honest."

Bea seriously doubted Burt would keep that promise. She watched until Jack escorted him out of the party, then she turned to Harrison. "I suppose that if the boy's high spirits could be turned to something useful, he might have quite an ingenious career at one thing or another."

"If he can avoid the gallows," Harrison said with a wry grin.

"I told you it wasn't me," John was in the middle of saying to Diana as Bea's attention was drawn toward the couple. "And here you thought I was such a villain."

"You are a villain," Diana insisted. She no longer stood in John's arms. In fact, everything about her countenance had changed to the complete opposite of what it had been minutes before. "You might not have been the one to pull those pranks at the orphanages, but I am quite certain that you are guilty of some sort of egregious sin."

"The only sin I'm guilty of is, well, it's unmentionable in present company." John glanced around at the party guests, who were slowly calming down and resuming their party activities. "But if you'd care to step into a quiet alcove with me, I can demonstrate every sin I'm capable of." He finished his teasing with a blatantly salacious wink.

Diana yelped and tilted her head up, her face flushing. She turned away from John and crossed her arms. "You are impossible. Utterly impossible."

"But you adore me anyhow," John said, sliding right up behind her, close enough that he could have nibbled on Diana's ear.

He might have tried just that. Diana leapt away from him so fast that she nearly stumbled. Her face went redder than ever, and the look she sent John over her shoulder before marching away was as much of a challenge for him to try and come after her as it was scolding for his bad behavior.

John glanced toward Bea and Harrison, saying, "It

appears as though hunting season has started," before following Diana across the room.

"The two of them are perfectly horrid," Harrison's grandmother said, hobbling her way over to where Bea and Harrison stood, frozen in perplexity at the odd turn the party had taken. "And they are deliciously entertaining to watch."

The band finished retuning their instruments after the fright and launched into a jolly Christmas tune. The air of panic that had encompassed the room gradually died down. Some of the young men who worked for various orphanages rushed forward to clean up the burnt papers and soot caused by Burt's firecrackers. All in all, the party was able to resume without much fuss. Some of the children, particularly the boys, were even laughing about the disruption and retelling the tale with their own embellishments. Bea was amazed at how quickly things could move on after a terrifying situation.

"I just hope that John doesn't cause too much trouble for himself where Diana is concerned," Harrison said, still hovering protectively close to Bea.

His grandmother laughed. "Young men are forever causing trouble for themselves where women are concerned. Particularly young men of title who are in love. Which brings me to you, my boy."

Harrison stiffened at Bea's side as his grandmother narrowed her gaze at him. "What about me?" he asked.

Bea found herself holding her breath as his grandmother said, "Your friend, Lord Whitlock, isn't the only one who should be proposing right about now. After the conversation we had on Monday, I was expecting news regarding Lady Beatrice here."

Bea had the feeling Harrison's grandmother had deliberately let out a secret. Her heart raced even faster than it had when the crackers went off.

"Why isn't my mother's ring gracing this delightful young woman's finger right now?" Harrison's grand- mother asked on. "I gave that ring to you on the under- standing that it wouldn't stay in your possession for long."

"Oh." Bea sucked in a breath and pressed a hand over her racing heart. She glanced from Harrison's grand- mother to Harrison himself, expectation making her dizzy.

Harrison let out a guilty breath, looking as though he'd rather be anywhere in England besides that room at that moment. "I did intend to propose," he said, wincing and looking at Bea. "I wanted it to be a surprise. I had such grand plans for the perfect proposal."

"They why didn't you make it?" his grandmother asked.

The color in Harrison's cheeks flushed deeper, and his guilty look seemed to spread to encompass him. "The fact is, Grandmama, I...I'm afraid I lost the ring."

"You lost it?" His grandmother flinched back, looking horrified, but not particularly surprised. A moment later, she shook her head and closed her eyes, pressing her fingertips to her forehead. "Oh, Harrison."

"I hoped that I could find it," Harrison explained. "I

lost it in this very room, the other day, when we were sorting donations for the orphanages. I put it on a table when I rushed to help Bea with decorations, and when I came back, the table had been cleared. The donations were taken to three separate orphanages, and John and I spent the next two days tracking them down and searching for the ring, but we had no luck."

A burst of hope that bordered on giddiness filled Bea's chest. "And one of those orphanages was Mr. Siddel's, wasn't it?" she asked, turning to Harrison.

Harrison blinked at her, then said, "Yes."

Bea couldn't suppress her giggle as she reached into the reticule still tied to her wrist. Harrison had asked her to dance so soon after she entered the party that she hadn't had a chance to put her reticule down. Now she was glad that she still had it as she drew out the small, linen sack Annie from Mr. Siddel's orphanage, had given her. She hadn't thought of it before, but its contents were the perfect size and shape to be a ring box.

"That girl, Annie, from Mr. Siddel's orphanage gave this to me the other day when she learned that you and I are friends," she said, laughter in serious danger of getting the best of her. She handed the sack over to Harrison. "She said it was found in the donations and that she over-heard Harrison saying he was searching for it. She gave it to me to give to you, which I intended to do this evening."

"Did you open it to see what it was?" Harrison asked, taking a velvet ring box from the sack.

Bea caught her breath at the sight of it. "No. It wasn't

mine. I had no right to meddle with something that belonged to you."

"Honest and noble to a fault," Harrison's grandmother said with a pleased smile.

Harrison opened the box and peeked at its contents, breaking into a relieved smile. He closed the box just as quickly, though, and lowered his hands.

A tickling wave of disappointment filled Bea. "I'm surprised she knew it belonged to you," she said, trying to mask her feelings over not receiving an instant proposal.

Harrison glanced at the bottom of the ring box, then showed it to Bea. "The family coat of arms and name are stamped on the box," he said.

Sure enough, the Landsbury sigil was there, plain for all to see.

"I'm glad that your heirloom was returned," Bea said, suddenly anxious. She swayed on her spot, glancing around for her friends, uncertain what she should do next. "I suppose you'll want to get on with the party now."

"What I would like," Harrison said, a mischievous smile spreading across his face, "is to have a private word with you, if I might, Lady Beatrice."

Tears sprung instantly to Bea's eyes, and for a moment she couldn't breathe. Joy burst through her as loud as any of the crackers Burt had set off. She couldn't speak, could only reply to Harrison's request by nodding quickly and taking his hand when he offered it to her.

With a final look for his grandmother—who nodded

approvingly and beamed from ear to ear—Harrison escorted Bea across the room of Christmas revelers as the band finished a lively song and began to play one of Bea's favorite, festive tunes. Harrison whisked her out of the crowded room, glanced around the building's front hallway, then tugged her off to the side, to a wide staircase. He led her up a flight and a half of stairs until they came to a wide window that looked out over the cozy, frost-covered street. The night was clear, and bright moonlight shone down from the dark sky. Even the flickering lights of the other buildings on the street loaned a feeling of magic and promise to the moment.

"Bea," Harrison said, fiddling nervously with the ring box as he gazed at her. "I knew I wanted to marry you from the first moment I met you at that ball, years ago."

That was all it took for Bea to burst into tears of joy. She gulped for breath and tried to remain calm as Harrison went on.

"I shouldn't have hesitated, not for a second. I don't even know why I did, except that I was having such a delightful time getting to know you and love you even more that I felt I didn't have a spare moment for anything else. But I am certain beyond a shadow of a doubt that you are the woman I want to spend the rest of my life with. I love you, Beatrice. I love you more than I thought my heart was capable of."

He took a step back, got down on one knee, and opened the ring box, presenting her with the diamond and emerald ring inside.

"Say you'll marry me, Bea," he said, his voice hoarse with emotion. "Say you'll be my wife."

Bea swallowed a sound of delight that came straight from the bottom of her soul and nodded so fast it made her dizzy. "Yes," she managed to squeak out. "Yes, of course I'll marry you."

Tears streamed down her face as Harrison got to his feet—crying a bit himself—and took the ring out of its box. He set the box on the windowsill before taking Bea's hand and sliding the ring onto her finger.

"Don't forget about that," Bea said through a sniffle, nodding to the discarded ring box on the windowsill. "We wouldn't want to lose it."

"Of course not," he said, sweeping her into his arms.

A moment later, the ring box was forgotten entirely as Harrison slanted his mouth over hers. It was the most beautiful and perfect kiss Bea had ever received. It was passionate and tender, filling her with joy and desire from her head to her toes. But more than that, it was perfect because of what it meant. It meant that, at long last, she would be Harrison's wife.

CHAPTER 10

The wedding day was everything Bea had ever imagined it would be and more. She and Harrison had seen no reason to wait after their engagement was finally official. Valentine's Day was the perfect day for a wedding between two people who loved each other so much. And while that hadn't left them much time to prepare for the day or to stage a wedding celebration to rival that of other aristocratic couples, Bea was perfectly fine with a small event.

Of course, that small event turned into something far more elaborate when word spread through the orphans that Bea and Harrison had worked so hard to help at Christmastime. Small gifts and cards wishing them well began to arrive weeks before the wedding, and when Bea had enough of them lining the mantle in her bedroom, she decided the only thing for it was to invite as many of the orphans as wanted to see what a society wedding was like to attend.

The result was that the modest church in Mayfair, where the Landsbury family had worshiped for generations, was packed to the rafters with eager young faces. Their eyes were wide with wonder as Bea made her way down the aisle, dressed in a gown of white lace, her veil as long as her train, a bouquet of roses in her hands.

"She looks like a princess," one of the orphan girls whispered as she passed her pew.

"No, she looks like an angel," another said in awe.

Bea grinned at their innocent joy. That grin became a smile of pure joy as she approached the altar, where Harrison stood, John at his side, serving as his best man. Diana was Bea's bridesmaid, of course. She stood across from John, doing an admirable job of not looking as though she wanted to tear his eyes out. In fact, for a change, Diana seemed not even to care that John was mere yards away, smiling at her instead of the bride. It was icing on the cake of what was turning into the perfect day.

All thoughts of her friends were cast aside as Bea stepped up to meet Harrison as the minister came forward. He was as handsome as she'd ever seen him, though that had less to do with his finely-tailored suit and everything to do with the joy that shone in his eyes. Finally, after what felt like a lifetime, and yet no time at all, there they were, facing each other in front of God and all of their friends and family.

The ceremony passed in a blur. All Bea was certain she would remember about it was the bliss she felt and the love that radiated from Harrison. She hoped she said her vows correctly, but even that didn't matter when the minister pronounced them man and wife. The happiness that filled Bea's heart then was like nothing she'd ever known and brought tears to her eyes. Those tears vanished in an instant, though, the moment Harrison kissed her for the first time as her husband.

The ceremony was lovely, but it was the reception afterwards that had Bea positively buzzing with joy.

"And to think," her father said, thumping Harrison on the back as he and Bea mingled with their guests. "I didn't even have to implement the thumb-screws or lecture the man about his profligate ways to get him to the altar at last."

"Again, my lord, I am terribly sorry that I behaved inappropriately with your daughter before Christmas," Harrison said, his face flushing. "You must know that I had only the most honorable intentions toward her."

"A little too honorable, if you ask me," Bea's father laughed. "Young people should be young and have a little fun. That's what life and love are all about."

Bea laughed, certain her father was only expressing

such progressive views now because she and Harrison were well and truly married at last. "Would you say the same about Evelyn?" she asked, teasing her father with a sly look.

"I suppose I would," her father said. "Today, I'm feeling rather magnanimous toward young people."

"Then I take it you don't care that Evelyn is currently conversing with Lord Meadowbrook," Bea said. She nodded across the room to where her sister was standing rather too close to one of London's most notorious bounders. The two of them had their heads together as though discussing some of the finer points of Valentine's Day entertainment.

Her father lost his jolly smile. He cleared his throat as his expression settled into a frown, then tugged at the cuffs of his jacket, as if preparing to do battle, before striding across the room to have a word with Lord Meadowbrook and Evelyn.

"Do you think your sister is in danger?" Harrison asked, bending close so he could speak quietly to her. In fact, Bea suspected that he bent close merely so that he could be closer to her and closer to a kiss.

"Evelyn? No," Bea laughed. "She's far too sensible to fall for the charms of a man like Lord Meadowbrook. But Papa will have a delightful time frightening the man out of his wits all the same."

Harrison laughed at her quip, resting a hand on the small of her back as they glanced around the room at their guests. "It looks as though someone else is running the risk of being frightened out of their wits by someone's parent," he said, nodding toward John and Diana at the other end of the room.

Diana had her back up, as usual, but that wasn't stopping John from leaning in to her and whispering something in her ear. He went so far as to curl a tendril of Diana's hair at the nape of her neck around his finger. Diana flinched, turning to him with a furious look. That look was heated in more ways than one, though. She leaned toward John, muttering something through a clenched jaw, fire in her eyes. Bea couldn't hear what she was saying, but whatever it was, it must have been lively. Diana's eyes were filled with fire.

"Is she telling him off or preparing to kiss him?" Harrison asked, his mouth twitching as though he wasn't sure whether he should laugh or not.

"It could be either," Bea said, just as amused. "It could be both."

"I wouldn't be the least bit surprised," Harrison said, giving up and laughing at last. "I also wouldn't be surprised if we had another wedding to attend this spring."

"Do you think they'll wait that long?" Bea asked with a wry look up at him.

"Do you know, I'm not sure they will," Harrison went on laughing. He nodded to Diana's mother, Lady Pickwick, who was watching Diana and John as though she were a police inspector about to make an arrest. "I have a feeling that if those two aren't exceptionally careful, they may find themselves in more hot water than they anticipated."

"Wouldn't that be wonderful," Bea said with an amused sigh. "It would put the rest of us out of our misery."

"Yes," Harrison agreed, his gaze shifting to her and turning amorous. "There's nothing more aggravating than watching two people who are obviously meant to be together dancing around each other and delaying the inevitable."

Bea's heart fluttered, both at his words and at the hungry way he studied her. They had been perfect angels around each other ever since the engagement. Aside from a handful of times when no one else was around and they'd stolen a few kisses that were far from chaste. The heat in Harrison's eyes spoke of something far more exciting now, something that was now not only allowed for them, but was expected. Bea had been dreaming of her wedding night for years, and now it had arrived.

"Do you think anyone would mind if we quietly slipped away from the party and made our way upstairs?" she asked in a whisper, giving Harrison what she hoped was a suggestive look. Seduction was such a new art form to her, but if she didn't start somewhere, she would never become an expert at it.

"I don't think they'd mind at all," Harrison replied,

arching one eyebrow invitingly. "In fact, if we snuck out of the room quietly, I don't think they'd even notice."

A giggle caught in Bea's throat as she pulled her eyes away from Harrison and glanced around the room, assessing who was there and how likely she and Harrison were to be able to cross the room, dash through the hall, and retreat upstairs without being noticed. She was certain that a hundred kinds of suspicion painted her face as Harrison took her hand and subtly glided across the room with her. Anyone who knew about those things was certain to see exactly what she and Harrison were up to as they avoided being drawn into conversations and made their way into the hall.

Whether anyone noticed them leaving and simply chose to let them go or whether they truly were as sneaky as they thought they were, they made it to the stairs without being ambushed by any guests and fled to the quiet security of the family quarters. Bea's things had all been moved to Landsbury House earlier in the week, and Harrison had moved from his old, bachelor's bedroom at the near end of the hall to one of the larger suites at the back of the hall.

"I think we pulled that off with grace and aplomb," he said breathlessly as they slipped into their new bedroom and shut the door behind them.

"Yes, we did," Bea answered, shivering inside over what came next.

There was no need to lock the door or care what the

servants would think. The power of marriage was enough to afford them all the privacy they needed, something Bea appreciated in the fullest as Harrison swept her into his arms.

"I love you, my perfect wife," he breathed before slanting his mouth over hers.

With all the practice she'd had in the last few weeks, Bea was still blown over by the deliciousness of Harrison's kiss. Her mouth felt as though it were made to meld with his. She loved the way he teased her lips with his own and with his teeth and tongue. She circled her arms around his back, holding on to what she loved most, as he slipped his tongue along hers, exploring her fully. There was so much beauty and so much power in something as simple as a kiss. It swirled through her, making her bold.

She brought her hands around to the front of his jacket, surprising herself with her dexterity as she worked open the buttons of his jacket and waistcoat. Once they were undone, she tugged his silky-smooth shirt out from the waist of his trousers.

Harrison made a sound of surprise and delight before breaking their kiss. "I had no idea my wife would be so eager," he said, his lips forming a smile as he tried to continue kissing her and talking at the same time.

"I've waited long enough." She laughed deep in her throat, then glanced up at him with a coquettish grin. "I'm not all sweetness and light, you know."

"I daresay you are quite a bit more," he said, his voice

rough with desire, shrugging out of his jacket and letting it drop to the side. "And I cannot wait to explore it all."

He reached his hands around her, tracing the line of buttons along her back. At the same time, he pulled her closer, kissing her with surprising levels of passion.

A moment later, he stepped back, amusement in his eyes. "Good Lord. How many buttons does this dress have anyhow?"

Bea giggled, pressing a hand to her kiss-swollen lips, and turned to show him her back. Indeed, the number of buttons that fastened her high-necked wedding gown in back was monumental.

Harrison let out an exaggerated sigh and went to work unfastening each and every one. "Something you will quickly discover about making love is that the most tedious part is removing clothes in order to enjoy the most intimate experience possible."

"You sound as though it's a harsh task," she laughed, prickles of expectation following the brush of his fingers as he made his way through her buttons.

"It is," he said with exaggerated displeasure. He leaned in close enough for her to feel his breath on her neck and said, "Especially when all you want is for you and your lover to be naked and entwined as fast as possible."

She shivered in earnest at his use of the word "lover". That was what they would be now. And he was right, she couldn't wait.

It seemed to take forever for him to get through the buttons of her gown, and once that was loosened, he still had all of the fastenings of her skirts and the fashionable bustle that went with them.

"Heavens, how much does this all weigh?" he asked once the ensemble was loosened enough for her to step out of.

"Far more than it appears," she said, rolling her eyes and picking her dress up off the floor to move it to a chaise near the window.

When she turned back, Harrison had not only shed his waistcoat and cravat, and toed out of his shoes, he had his shirt most of the way over his head, exposing the broad expanse of his bare chest. Bea sucked in a breath at the sight. He was so well-formed, exceeding the expectations of what she would find under his clothes when the moment finally came.

"That's not fair at all," she gasped as she paused to sit on the chaise so that she could quickly remove her shoes. When she stood, she tugged frantically at the ties holding her petticoats on.

"What isn't?" Harrison laughed, discarding his shirt, then practically stalking across the room to her, like a ravenous wolf who had spotted prey.

Bea fought to keep her wits about her instead of melting into a wanton pool of jelly as she stepped out of her skirts and into Harrison's arms. "It's so much easier for men to remove their clothes than it is for women."

"It's because men are hopeless beasts," Harrison growled against her ear, sliding his hands across her still-corseted torso and closing a hand over one of her breasts.

Bea had the feeling he'd intended to say something more, but before he could, he kissed her cheek, which turned into kissing her neck, which turned into trailing kisses across her shoulder to the swell of her breast. She gasped and shivered at the sensations—not only where he kissed her, but the ache that grew and grew in her core. Everything she'd ever been told about relations between men and women suddenly made sense. She was certain beyond a shadow of a doubt that she wouldn't have resisted him one bit if he'd kissed and held and touched her this way months ago, or even the night they'd met. Her body felt as though it was made to be with his this way.

"Now, let's just take care of the rest of these pesky things," he growled, sliding his hands to the fastenings of her corset.

There were more hooks and buttons and ties to undo than Bea had the patience for. It was as though her clothing had grown more fastenings just so that it would take Harrison longer to peel the layers of her fine things off. They did come off, one by one, though. She dropped each item aside without a care in the world until, at last, she stood naked in his arms, shivering with expectation.

"Are you cold?" he asked in a rumbling voice, sliding his arms around her. "I can warm you up."

"I'm certain you can," she said, eyes fixed on his lips.

She lifted to her toes, leaning into him and kissing him with all the need that was mounting inside of her. She felt far less anxious about being naked in his arms than she thought she would, particularly as his chest felt so warm and firm against hers. She snaked her arms around him, holding him even closer and digging her fingertips into his back as he kissed her hard. She moaned in response, ready to give him everything and then some.

When she arched her hips into his, feeling his hardness through his trousers, it was as though something clicked inside of him. He lifted her fully into his arms so that she could wrap her legs around him, and he carried her quickly to the bed. He deposited her there with almost comical enthusiasm, then stepped back to fumble his way out of his trousers.

Bea giggled and scurried to pull back the bedcovers, but she stopped with a gasp as he kicked his trousers aside and stood, his erection on full display. She'd thought she would be terrified of that part of him, especially after hearing the tales her aunt had told her in preparation for her wedding night, but, in fact, she was captivated.

"I'll be careful," Harrison promised as he crawled onto the bed with her, maneuvering her to her back between the sheets. "I know the first time can be difficult for a woman but—"

She stopped his nonsense with a kiss, molding her

lips to his as her hand reached between them to touch him. They both groaned as soon as she made contact, filling her hand with him and marveling at how hard and hot he was. Touching him that way was a revelation. She only wished she could look at him as she explored him, learning the length of his shaft and the strange shape of its tip. Hunger grew inside of her like nothing she'd ever known as he shifted restlessly against her touch, teaching her how to stroke him.

Far too soon, he stopped her, laughing deep in his throat, and deliberately moved her hand to pin it to the mattress beside them. "If you keep that up, love, I'll embarrass myself by failing to last more than a minute."

"We wouldn't want that," she hummed, wriggling against him and reveling in every sensation that caused.

"I can see you're going to be the death of me," he laughed, bending down to kiss her again.

She had a reply ready, but it floated clear out of her head as he kissed her. Kissing while upright and clothed was one thing, but kissing naked and horizontal was something else entirely. Bea decided in an instant that she loved it. She traced her hands up and down his sides, learning the feel of his strong body, and opened her hips so that she could cradle him against the part of her that wanted him the most.

She must have been doing everything right to please him, because his breath came in shorter and shorter gasps and the tension rippling from him was palpable. He broke from her mouth to kiss his way to her breasts. In a flash, it was her turn to wonder how long she could stand the pleasure he gave her as he kissed and nipped first one breast, then the other, laving his tongue over her nipples in turn, until they were tight points of pleasure. She'd never imagined anything could feel so good.

Within moments, he showed her that there were things that could feel even better as he slipped one hand between her legs.

"So wet," he groaned as he stroked her in the most intimate way possible.

A faint voice in the back of Bea's mind wondered if that was something she should be embarrassed about. That voice was utterly silenced as he slipped first one, then two fingers inside of her. She let out a wanton moan and pressed into his hand as he surprised her with intense pleasure. Her body was so eager for him that the wild, powerful sensations he coaxed out of her took up every free space in her mind. Those sensations towered to heights of pleasure she had only dreamed of when he circled and stroked her clitoris, causing her body to burst into waves of pure bliss.

It was wonderful and beautiful, and made even more so as she shared it with him. Her sighs mingled with his groan of victory, which quickly turned to more as he repositioned himself between her legs and plunged into her. Bea had been warned that her first time would be painful, and perhaps one of the sensations she felt was pain, but it was eclipsed a thousand times by the joy of being filled by him. It was such a new and captivating feeling that she gasped, clinging to him.

Harrison paused, glancing down at her. "Are you all right? Did I hurt you?"

"Why did you stop?" she panted, wriggling against him and encouraging him to go on.

A smile of absolute adoration spread across his face as he resumed his thrusts. He gazed down at her, transfixed by what he saw, then picked up the pace and intensity of his movements. The connection Bea felt between them went far beyond any vows that could ever have been spoken in church. This was their benediction, and when Harrison's thrusts turned frantic and blossomed into a sound of pure joy as his body tensed then released, Bea knew they were well and truly one soul.

The cozy bliss that followed, as they collapsed together in what felt like a puddle of arms and legs and satisfaction, was as wonderful as the pitched feelings of need that had encompassed them minutes before.

"I love you so," Bea panted, curling her body around his as he caught his breath beside her. "I've never been happier than this moment."

"I love you," he echoed her. His face split into a grin. "And I can assure you that there are many more happy moments to come."

I HOPE YOU HAVE ENJOYED BEA AND HARRISON's story! At last, true love triumphs! But what about Diana and John? Are they really enemies or will they be lovers at last? And will Diana give in and admit she loves him or will the fates and outside sources have to intervene? Find out next in *How to Avoid a Scandal* (*Or Not*), available now! Keep clicking to get a jump on reading Chapter One...

IF YOU ENJOYED THIS BOOK AND WOULD LIKE TO HEAR more from me, please sign up for my newsletter! When you sign up, you'll get a free, full-length novella, *A Passionate Deception*. Victorian identity theft has never been so exciting in this story of hope, tricks, and starting over. Part of my *West Meets East* series, *A Passionate Deception* can be read as a stand-alone. Pick up your free copy today by signing up to receive my newsletter (which I only send out when I have a new release)!

Sign up here: http://eepurl.com/cbaVMH

ARE YOU ON SOCIAL MEDIA? I AM! COME AND JOIN the fun on Facebook: http://www. facebook.com/merryfarmerreaders

. . .

I'M ALSO A HUGE FAN OF INSTAGRAM AND POST LOTS of original content there: https://www. instagram.com/merryfarmer/

## AND NOW TO GET STARTED ON HOW TO AVOID A SCANDAL (OR NOT)...

*LONDON – MAY, 1888*

SHE HATED HIM. LADY DIANA PICKWICK HATED Lord John Darrow, Viscount Whitlock, with the fire of a thousand suns. She hated him when she woke up in the morning, as she went about her business during the day, paying calls and attending to the various political causes the May Flowers championed, and she hated him when she went to bed at night.

He was standing across the large salon the May Flowers had rented for their political rally and tableau of powerful women in history, looking as smug as you please in his expertly tailored suit. The fashionable lines of the jacket accented John's broad shoulders and trim waist. The way he moved as he laughed over something one of his friends said showed off the power in his fine frame. His dark eyes danced with mischief, and he brushed a hand through his thick, chestnut locks as he composed himself after his laughter. The strong set of his jaw formed a perfect contrast to his sensual lips.

Not that Diana noticed any of that. She cleared her throat and dragged her eyes back to the podium she was arranging for the day's speeches. She hated John Darrow. He was a menace and a rogue. He'd teased her mercilessly for over two years now, always singling her out for pranks and games at the gatherings their friends held. He winked at her and flirted with her, whether she wanted it or not, even in public. He vexed her at every turn, treating her the way a man would treat a barmaid at his favorite pub instead of taking her seriously. She was the leader of the May Flowers, after all. She had a right to be treated with respect. Something John failed to do in even the smallest way with his flashing eyes and his expressive mouth and his—

"Good heavens, Diana. If you keep staring at the man like that, you're likely to cause his clothes to combust and fall right off of him," Lady Bianca Clerkenwell said, startling Diana out of her thoughts.

"I beg your pardon?" she asked, her voice coming out breathless and strangled. She hadn't heard Bianca approach, hadn't noticed her sister, Natalia Townsend, with her, and likely wouldn't have noticed if the roof had caved in, raining puppies on them all.

Bianca grinned knowingly, patting Diana's arm with a look of mock sympathy. "There, there," she said, barely keeping her laughter—or her ribald sense of humor—in check. "If you want to lure the man into marriage, all you need to do is follow those sultry looks with sultry actions."

"I do not—how could you suggest—John Darrow is the last man on earth that I would want to take tea with, let alone marry," Diana snapped. She might have stomped her foot as she avowed it as well.

Bianca and Natalia exchanged an amused look, their eyes sparkling with mirth.

"Marriage is actually quite lovely," Natalia said. "Linus and I enjoy it very much."

"And heaven knows Jack and I are fond of the institution," Bianca added. She smoothed a hand over her stomach. "Perhaps a little too fond."

Natalia whipped to face her. "Again?"

Bianca sent her sister a sheepish look. "As if you're one to talk."

Natalia sucked in a breath, her eyes going wide. "You aren't supposed to know about that yet," she whispered.

"Darling, it's written all over your face," Bianca said.

Their conversation was interrupted as Diana's closest friend, Lady Beatrice Manfred, skipped over to join them by the podium. Bea practically glowed with excitement, her cheeks rosy and her eyes bright. Diana instantly dreaded what could have put such joy on Bea's face.

"I'm so happy to have found you all here," Bea said, grabbing Diana's arm and giggling. "I wanted you all, my dearest friends, to be the first to know." She, too, dropped a hand to her stomach.

"No." Diana shook her head, peeling Bea's hand away from her arm. "No, I refuse to hear it. Not you too."

"Me too?" Bea blinked, her mirth turning to confusion.

Bianca raised one hand with a laugh. "It seems Natalia and I are in good company."

Bea's smile returned full force. "The two of you as well?"

Natalia grasped Bea's hand and giggled. "Do you suppose all three of us will give birth in the same month? Oh, how lovely to think our children will all be of an age and grow up together! Perhaps, if one is a boy and another is a girl, they might even marry someday."

That was the final straw, as far as Diana was concerned. No, the final straw was when she glanced across the room as a means to escape her friends' joy and found John staring right at her with that wicked little grin of his. As if he knew what sort of news her friends were sharing. As if he wanted to make it four pregnancies instead of three. How dare the bastard grin at her so blatantly in public? He made her feel so...so...so....

She huffed out a breath and turned back to her friends. "Many felicitations on your happy conditions," she said in clipped tones. "Now, if you will excuse me, some of us have chosen to continue the fight for the rights of women rather than sliding into tired old patterns of motherhood."

Diana knew the moment the words were past her lips that she sounded peevish and bitter. Her friends didn't deserve that. Fortunately—or perhaps very much unfortunately—all three of them looked at her with sympathy and understanding.

"Your time will come soon, darling. Just you wait," Bianca said.

"You sound exactly like my mother," Diana growled. "Don't let her hear you talking."

"Is she here?" Bianca glanced around.

"She is, and Papa too," Diana sighed. "As though I am a child giving a recital that they have to attend."

"Then I'll just go have a word with them and suggest ways they can make your time come sooner," Bianca teased her.

"I do not want my time to come at all," Diana insisted in reply. "I have only ever had one aim in life, and that is to be a strong, independent, powerful woman, like the women we will be portraying in today's tableau."

"Yes, I suppose we should all don our costumes for that," Bea said. "It's too early for any of the audience to know they are watching three women in a delicate condition."

"At least three," Natalia said. "I heard that Cynthia Withers is expecting as well."

"Oh?" Bianca raised one eyebrow, sending a concerned look Diana's way. She slipped her arm around her sister's back and gently led her to the curtain that separated the area where the podium stood from the backstage area, where the tableau was being set up. "Do tell me all about it."

Diana watched them go, doing her best to maintain an air of strength and fortitude. One final look of compassion from Bea before she, too, slipped backstage had Diana's heart sagging. She fussed with the notes for her speech that sat on the podium, trying to chase the gloom from her heart.

She was the last of her friends who remained unmarried. In the past few years, she'd watched each of them—from Cecelia Marlowe years ago to Bea just a few months prior—walk down the aisle to marry good men. Even Freddy Harrington and Reese Howsden had discreetly taken up with each other and were now raising a foundling girl, along with Reese's son, Harry, though she wasn't supposed to know the scandalous truth of their romance. It all made Diana feel very much like a dusty old doll that had been put on a back shelf, never to be played with again. She was hard-pressed to find men who would so much as waltz with her when she attended balls anymore, let alone ones who would walk out with her.

Not that she wanted to walk out with any man.

She shot a look straight across the room to John, her eyes narrowing. It was all John's fault. He monopolized her time, both in public and in private. How was she supposed to draw the attention of anyone else when he constantly loomed over her the way he did? It wasn't as though he had any intentions toward her other than his attempts to drive her mad.

Her heart thudded miserably over that thought in a way that felt distinctly like yearning.

No, that was wrong. She did not want John Darrow. She did not want him in any way at all.

She cleared her throat and called out, "Ladies and gentlemen! Ladies and gentlemen, please give me the honor of your attention."

The room quieted with surprising speed. Diana had always possessed a powerful voice that demanded people listen to her. She wasn't ignorant of the way her striking beauty held attention either. But if she was so very beautiful, why was she the last of her friends to snag a husband?

She instantly pushed that thought aside with a bout of fury at herself. At least that fury was useful when it came to expounding on the cause that meant so much to her.

"Ladies and gentlemen, we are here today to celebrate the strength and power of women throughout the ages," she began, standing tall and meeting the eyes of as many of the men and women in her audience as she could. When she met John's eyes as he stared at her with a grin, arms crossed, she tilted her chin up farther and went on. "You all know that the goal of the May Flowers is to fight for women's right to vote. The right to have our voice heard and to have our opinions counted in matters of government is exceedingly important. For it is our leaders that decide our fates. To be denied the right to have a say in who those leaders are is scandalous.

"But I want to speak to you today about something that I believe is equally as important," she went on, shifting to grip the edges of the podium. She stared particularly at the women in the audience as she said, "Ladies, though it is not a topic we are encouraged to think of, each and every one of you should turn your attention to your financial independence."

A surprised murmur passed through the room. It was precisely the sort of reaction Diana had expected for her unusual topic.

"That is right, my friends," she continued. "Several years ago, in eighteen eighty-two, our allies in Parliament passed the Married Women's Property Act. Among other things, this forward-thinking parliamentary measure has given us the right to conduct our business as our own. We no longer need the permission or the supervision of our husbands, fathers, or brothers to maintain and grow our own finances. Our income does not automatically become the property of our husbands when we marry, and I, for one, think it is essential that we make the most of that."

Judging by the mutters and hums of the audience, Diana would have thought she'd called for a revolution. She loved the zip of tension her suggestion brought with it, though, so she went on with enthusiasm.

"Now is the time, ladies, to educate yourselves about matters of money and investments. Now is the time to search out financial opportunities and to increase your own bank accounts. Women should no longer be reliant on pin money provided to us by the men in our lives. For the first time ever, we have it within our power to support ourselves on our own income. I believe this is the single most important step a woman can take to secure herself and her future. It is not the pen that is mightier than the sword, it is the pound."

She finished her speech with a triumphant smile and was rewarded with enthusiastic applause from many of the ladies present. The applause from the rest of the room was somewhat less enthusiastic, and a few of the gentlemen in attendance looked downright offended Diana sought out John to see what he thought, but the blighter was already in conversation with his friends, Bea's husband, Harrison, and Freddy and Reese. Diana tried not to take it personally, but it stung that he wasn't paying attention to her.

No, that wasn't right. She didn't give a fig what John Darrow thought of her.

"And now," she went on, "in a few moments' time, the ladies of the May Flowers would like to present to you our tableau of powerful women throughout history."

A renewed smattering of applause followed as Diana stepped away from the podium and headed backstage. She needed to change into her costume depicting the Greek goddess Athena as quickly as possible, as she was one of the first scenes in the tableau. As pleased as she'd been with her idea earlier, it felt hollow now. She was filled with brave words about how women should live their lives—and her own financial portfolio was an impressive example of living up to her words—but more often than not, she felt as though she were fighting a losing battle against forces that hadn't changed for hundreds of years and wouldn't change anytime soon.

## WANT TO READ MORE?
## PICK UP HOW TO AVOID A SCANDAL (OR NOT) TODAY!

Click here for a complete list of other works by Merry Farmer.

# AFTERWORD

Are you looking for some other fun Christmas stories to read? Check out *The Holiday Hussy*, part of my *When the Wallflowers were Wicked*, fun and irreverent Regency romance series!

Here's a little taste of Chapter One to get you started....

*Somerset, England – December, 1815*

Cold. Lady Alice Marlowe was freezing cold and huddled in the corner of her seat in the hired carriage that bumped and jostled along the frozen lane, heading toward Holly Manor. She could barely feel her fingers, and her toes had long since gone numb. It didn't matter how tightly she pulled her shawl around her, the thread-bare thing simply wasn't thick enough to provide adequate protection against the chill, December air.

"Stop fidgeting," Alice's father, Lord James Marlowe, the Earl of Stanhope, growled on the seat across from her. "You're making my head ache."

"Y-yes, F-father," Alice whispered through chattering teeth.

Her father looked just as cold as she did, but everything Alice knew about him told her he would rather die than admit to it. James Marlowe never admitted to anything. He refused to admit that his lands were in shambles because of his mismanagement. He refused to admit that, with only three daughters to his name, his title was on the verge of passing to his brother, Alice's delightful Uncle Richard. He refused to admit that the three marriages he'd arranged for his daughters at the house party at Hadnall Heath, home of Lord Rufus and Lady Caroline Herrington, were bad ones. And he most certainly refused to admit that Alice's younger sister, Imogen, had run off with Lord Thaddeus Herrington to avoid marrying her father's choice of groom.

"I said stop fidgeting," he snapped, grimacing at Alice without a shred of compassion for the cold. "Women should be invisible except when a man needs them to do their duty."

Alice gulped. "Yes, Father," she said, lowering her head.

"This spate of temper on your part is disgusting," he went on as though she had protested instead of meekly obeyed. "Count Fabian Camoni is an excellent match. His fame as a designer of gardens is known throughout

England and the continent. And as soon as the mess Bonaparte has created in Italy is resolved, he will possess vast lands in Tuscany, which I understand are incredibly profitable."

Alice bit her tongue, knowing that anything she said would be taken the wrong way. Her father was desperate for money and the appearance that he was a man of importance and influence. Imogen had failed to help his cause by eloping with Lord Thaddeus, her older sister, Lettuce, had been married off to a wealthy but miserly merchant who had surprised them all by declaring he would take his bride and his fortune off to America without so much as a cent for their father, and so the entire burden of fulfilling their father's aims had landed squarely on Alice's shoulders.

He rubbed his hands together, but whether at the thought of the money he stood to gain through Alice's marriage or to ward off the cold, Alice didn't know. "Christmas is the perfect time to solidify this alliance," he went on. "It's a time of giving gifts and generosity. Not only will your groom give me the dowry price we agreed on, I'm certain I can squeeze more gold out of him. The fact that his mother remarried the Duke of Bolton is merely icing on the Christmas pudding. Bolton is drip-ping with money, and I have it on good authority that he's generous with his friends. This entire Christmas house party proves it."

"I thought the party was to celebrate the wedding," Alice said carefully. The last thing she wanted was to give her father the impression that she was blissfully going along with his plans. In fact, if she could have wrenched open the door and thrown herself out into the cold and barren landscape to avoid the whole thing, she would have.

Her father glared at her. "Arrogant chit," he hissed. "This endeavor is not about you."

Alice's eyes widened a fraction. Her own wedding was not about her? But of course, it wasn't. Her father would have required a heart to understand that marriages were supposed to be about love and companionability. They were supposed to contain passion, or at least mild attraction. And it wasn't as though she found Count Camoni unattractive. He'd been the prize catch of the house party with his rugged good looks and the aura of fame that surrounded him. Half of the young ladies at the party had flocked to him, gazing with open admiration at his broad shoulders and muscular frame, honed from all of the gardening work he did as part of his designs. They'd sighed over his blue eyes and blonde hair, which was unfashionably long, but glorious all the same. It wasn't his appearance or even his manners that filled Alice with dread and melancholy, it was the fact that she'd had no choice at all in the match. That and the fact that she hadn't seen him once since becoming engaged to him and had only had two letters in the five months since then.

"You will do your duty," her father went on in a lecturing tone. "After your marriage on Christmas Day, you will spread your legs eagerly for your husband so that he can get you with child as quickly as possible. An heir is the best way to ensure our families are entangled for all time."

Alice blushed with embarrassment at the mention of the marriage bed. She wasn't ignorant of those things, not after the Herrington's house party and the little souvenir she and her sisters had taken home and split between them. She wasn't even averse to them either. Part of her was exceptionally curious about matters of intimacy. But the thought of going to bed with Count Camoni because it was her duty, the idea that there was no point to the act but to produce an heir so that her father could sink his claws into Count Camoni's wealth, left her cold. Or perhaps that was merely the chill in the air.

Her father crossed his arms tightly and sank back into his seat, staring sullenly out the window at the frosty, Somerset countryside. The deep lines on his face hinted he had lapsed into thought and calculations about how he could increase his own fortunes. Alice waited, holding her breath, until she was relatively certain he wasn't paying attention to her any longer. Then she reached into the small satchel sitting on the seat beside her and drew out a book.

It wasn't a whole book. In fact, it was a third of one. When she and her sisters had discovered *The Secrets of Love* in a locked chest at the Herrington house party, it had felt as though they'd won a hunt for treasure. The volume contained everything any young woman could ever have wanted to know about the facts and fancies of love. Unlike most of the chaste and sedate books on the subject she had read before, *The Secrets of Love* contained vivid descriptions of the most sensual acts, interspersed between advice on how to find and keep a lover. Alice and her sisters had read the book so many times immediately after the house party that the spine had cracked. When each of their marriages were arranged and it became evident that the three of them would be split up, possibly never to see each other again, they'd divided the book in three, each of them taking a section.

Alice's middle section had no bindings, and it'd been all she could do to keep the pages from being damaged. She took one last peek at her father, and when she was certain he was distracted, she opened it to the chapter where she'd left off reading the night before. She already had most of the words memorized, but there was comfort in reading them again.

*"Love does not come with a sudden burst, like a man spending himself too soon only to fade and lose interest. It should unfold gradually, like a flower. First comes attraction, then intrigue, then titillation. Just as a lover undresses one article of clothing at a time or a gift is unwrapped bit by bit, the experience should be savored. By drawing out the process of love and reveling in each moment as it comes, passion and pleasure are increased, making the final blossoming all the more enjoyable."*

Alice sighed, warming from the inside out. She

could only imagine what it would be like to undress slowly for a lover, to make love the way she would savor a piece of cake instead of harshly lying back and parting her legs, like her father seemed to think she should do. Whoever the author of *The Secrets of Love* was, she— and Alice and her sisters were convinced the author was a woman—knew what a woman's heart longed for. And if there was one thing Alice's heart longed for, it was—

"What is that mangy pile of rubbish you're reading?" Her father snapped her out of her thoughts.

"It's nothing," Alice said with a gulp, slamming the pages closed and pushing the book back into her satchel before her father could read any of it.

"Don't you lie to me, you useless girl," he father growled.

"It's an instructional manual." Alice scrambled for an answer her father would believe and that wouldn't result in him taking the book from her. "About the duties of marriage. Lettuce, Imogen, and I were all given a copy after our engagements." It was marginally true, but Alice held her breath all the same.

"Who gave it to you?" her father asked, suspicion narrowing his eyes.

Alice had to lie. "Uncle Richard. He said it would improve our immortal souls."

Her father continued to glare, but he didn't comment. If there was anyone in the world that he feared, it was his younger brother. Uncle Richard was an army officer and a commanding presence. Her father didn't dare say a cross word against him.

"It's useless for women to read," he grumbled. "There's no point in improving what cannot be improved, and anything else is frivolous waste. But never mind. We're here."

Blessedly, the carriage rolled to a stop in front of an enormous house. Alice hadn't realized they'd crossed onto the grounds of Holly Manor, but as she looked out when a footman raced down to open the carriage door, she was amazed by what she saw. The house itself was only fifty years old, but it had a gravity to it. At that moment, however, it was decorated for Christmas, with candles in the windows, boughs of pine and the holly that gave the estate its name strewn over the main door and front-facing windows, and cheery red bows adorning all.

Alice's father exited the carriage without looking back at her. Alice had to wait for the footman to hand her down. The rush of icy air that swirled around her made her teeth chatter, but the short line of Count Camoni's family and step-family waiting for them near the front door promised warmth to come.

"Hurry along, girl," her father growled, marching up the gravel path that crunched under his feet. He headed straight for the Duke of Bolton himself. "Good day, Your Grace." He smiled as though the world were filled with sunshine and light, as though he were a man prone to smiling.

"Lord Stanhope," the duke greeted him in return.

"Welcome to our home. I trust you had a pleasant journey?"

"It was excellent," her father lied.

He continued his conversation with the duke, oblivious to all else, including Alice making her way toward the line of people at the front door, her limbs stiff with cold.

"This must be Lady Alice," a matronly woman came forward to greet her with an eager smile. Alice assumed at once that she was the duchess, Count Camoni's mother. "Oh dear, you look chilled through. Do come inside."

"Y-your grace." Alice managed a painful curtsy as she approached the woman. A second, much younger woman stood behind her, smiling at Alice with eager eyes. Behind her stood Count Camoni himself.

Alice nearly stumbled at the shock of seeing her betrothed again after so long. He was taller than she remembered, his shoulders broader and the power radiating from him stronger. He smiled at her as though she were a tasty morsel newly arrived for him to devour. Everything *The Secrets of Love* had taught her about the ways a man looked at a woman he wanted rushed back to her and she quivered on the inside, and not from fear.

"Georgette and I will have you warm and cozy in no time," the duchess went on.

The other young woman, Georgette, rushed to Alice's side, putting an arm around her and drawing her toward the house. "Goodness, you are cold," she said, then added, "I'm Lady Georgette Farnsworth. The duke is my father and your fiancé, Count Camoni, is my step-brother."

"Oh," Alice said, too overwhelmed to say more. She blinked at the attractive young woman, her rosy cheeks and her friendly eyes, gaped at the house as they passed through the front door and into an enormous hall decorated with exquisite artwork and suits of armor, and caught her breath as Georgette escorted her into a parlor across the hall where a cheery blaze crackled in a festively-decorated hearth. Everything around her was beautiful and expensive, and the people who flooded into the parlor with them were lofty and well-mannered. Alice knew in an instant that she was in well over her head. And that was before Count Camoni approached her.

She was every bit as lovely as he remembered her to be. The moment Fabian laid eyes on his bride, he recalled all the reasons he had been so amenable to accepting her father's suggestion of marriage that summer. Alice was like a breath of fresh, spring air in, well, December. Although, she did look frozen through as his step-sister led her to the fireplace in the Forest Parlor. The cold had brought bright pink to her otherwise pale cheeks, and if he wasn't mistaken, the buttons standing out under the fabric of her too-thin bodice weren't buttons at all. He would never understand ladies' fashion and the inadequacy of the fabrics used these days. Alice should have been wearing a pelisse at the very least.

It had only begun to dawn on him that perhaps it wasn't Alice's intention to dress so scantily and that, in fact, something else was behind the too-light clothing she wore, judging by the way she huddled near the fire, looking as though she might weep with relief, when Lord Stanhope stepped up to his side.

"Count Camoni," he said in an irritatingly ingratiating voice. "How nice to see you again."

Fabian dragged his attention away from his bride to accept his soon-to-be father-in-law's outstretched hand. "Lord Stanhope," he said, the feeling that Lord Stanhope's outstretched hand was asking for money settling over him. "I'm glad to see you and Lady Alice have arrived safely."

"I've delivered her into your hands, sir," Lord Stanhope said with a sly smile. "I trust the wedding will take place soon and we can settle on the bride price."

Fabian blinked in shock at the abruptness of Lord Stanhope's words. If it weren't for the fact that he truly did find Alice to be everything he wanted in a woman, he never would have entered into any sort of agreement to attach himself to the man. "Everything is in order," he answered without a smile. "But if you will excuse me, I would like to greet my bride."

"Yes, yes. You do that," Lord Stanhope said, thumping him on the back when he turned toward Alice.

Fabian frowned over his shoulder as he crossed the

room. He caught the eye of his step-brother, Lord Matthew Farnsworth. The two were roughly the same age and had gotten along famously from the moment Fabian's mother had married Matthew's father. They exchanged a look of brotherly knowing before Fabian reached the fireside and Alice.

"Lady Alice," Fabian greeted his vision of loveliness with a warm smile. "It is a joy and a pleasure to see you again."

To Fabian's disappointment, Alice glanced down, dipping into a short, polite curtsy before saying, "My lord," with all the disinterest of a child forced to sit through a particularly dull sermon.

Fabian's brow twitched as he scrambled to think of something more inviting to say. "I'm happy to see you looking so well. I thought the summer sun was becoming to you, but the coziness of a winter fire does just as much justice to your beauty."

She was silent, not meeting his eyes, shaking slightly, but whether from the cold or from something more sinister, Fabian couldn't tell. At last, she mumbled, "You are too kind."

Fabian's initial enthusiasm flattened to wary concern. "Are you well?" he asked. "You look a bit cold. Perhaps the journey was too taxing for you?"

"I am perfectly well, my lord." She snapped her eyes up to meet his with a look of tight frustration. Her hands clutched the satchel she carried to the point where her knuckles went white.

Worry took over entirely from the eagerness Fabian had felt while watching her carriage roll up the drive. Something was wrong, but he couldn't imagine what it was. Unless....

"Please forgive me for not writing more often," he said in a quieter, more intimate voice. "I have had quite a few commissions to design winter gardens and green-houses all across England this autumn. And the business of my father's family's estate in Tuscany has preoccupied me to an unforgivable degree. I swear, I will make it up to you by lavishing you with attention during this holiday party, before and after our marriage." He added a mischievous flicker of his eyebrows on the off chance that a hint of sensuality would thaw her icy demeanor.

"As you wish, my lord," she muttered, glancing down.

Fabian opened his mouth to say more, but he couldn't think of a blasted thing to say. Ladies usually adored him, though it was awkward to even think it. Apparently, he had a combination of good looks, good fortune, and exoticism that sent female hearts fluttering. Alice's was the only heart he cared to make flutter since the house party that summer, though. She'd been so free and curious then. Now he wasn't certain who she was.

"Perhaps," he began slowly, glancing to Georgette, "you would like to retire to the room we have prepared for you?" He lifted his eyebrows with the question. "There you might warm yourself by a fire or under layers of down quilts."

At last, she looked up at him with a measure of gratitude. "Thank you, my lord. That would be nice."

"Come along," Georgette said, looping an arm around Alice's waist and nudging her forward. "I'll show you where you will be staying. I made certain Mama assigned you a room overlooking the garden. It's decorated in splendid fashion for the season."

Fabian stepped aside and watched as Georgette walked Alice out of the room. Lord Stanhope paused in the middle of what looked like an invasive conversation with the duke to stare at Georgette with open interest. He went so far as to absent-mindedly wipe his mouth, as if spotting a tasty morsel. Fabian kept his smile in place until Alice and Georgette disappeared around the corner, then let it drop into a troubled scowl. Lord Stanhope could be a problem if he latched onto Georgette.

"I thought you said Lady Alice was agreeable," Matthew said, stepping up beside him and tugging his thoughts back to his initial problem.

"She is," Fabian told him with a frown. "At least, she was this summer in Shropshire."

"Something must have happened between then and now," Matthew speculated, fingering the holly that decorated the mantel over the fire.

Fabian hummed, considering that. "I really shouldn't have been so distant with her once the engagement was settled."

"What could you have done?" Matthew shrugged. "You've been in high demand for over a year now, though why people hire a half-Italian to design gardens for them is beyond me." He grinned.

Fabian smiled at his friend's teasing. "Designing gardens is a fair sight better than idling around, waiting for your father to die so you can become a duke."

Matthew laughed and nodded toward his father. "The old man isn't going to keel over any time soon. Your mother has infused him with new life."

Fabian arched a brow warily. "I'd rather not know what my mother gets up to behind closed doors." He shifted his stance, studying his mother and the duke with a thoughtful look all the same. "They may have the right way of things, though."

"How do you mean?" Matthew asked.

Fabian crossed his arms and rubbed his chin. "Your father put on quite a show to woo my mother. I never had a chance to do the same with Lady Alice."

"And all women love to be wooed," Matthew added.

"They do. And perhaps that's why Lady Alice was so cold just now. Perhaps the key thing is for me to spend the next few days before the wedding truly wooing her, making her feel special."

"Of course." Matthew laughed as if it were obvious. "You need to fall prostrate at her feet and worship the ground she walks on. You need to show her that you want to marry her because she is a goddess and you want to be in her temple at all times." He added a ribald wink to his comment.

"I wouldn't mind pouring out daily libations on the

altar of her inner sanctum," Fabian agreed, equally lascivious.

"So do you know what you're going to do to win her?" Matthew asked.

Fabian glanced to the side, out the window, to spot the greenhouse he was in the middle of redesigning as an overdue wedding gift for his mother. "I have a few ideas," he said. "All it will take is a little plotting and a little magic."

Ready for more? You can purchase The Holiday Hussy here!

# ABOUT THE AUTHOR

I hope you have enjoyed *'Twas the Night Before Scandal*. If you'd like to be the first to learn about when new books in the series come out and more, please sign up for my newsletter here: http://eepurl.com/cbaVMH And remember, Read it, Review it, Share it! For a complete list of works by Merry Farmer with links, please visit http://wp.me/P5ttjb-14F.

Merry Farmer is an award-winning novelist who lives in suburban Philadelphia with her cats, Torpedo, her grumpy old man, and Justine, her hyperactive new baby. She has been writing since she was ten years old and realized one day that she didn't have to wait for the teacher to assign a creative writing project to write something. It was the best day of her life. She then went on to earn not one but two degrees in History so that she would always have something to write about. Her books have reached the Top 100 at Amazon, iBooks, and Barnes & Noble, and have been named finalists in the prestigious RONE and Rom Com Reader's Crown awards.

# ACKNOWLEDGMENTS

I owe a huge debt of gratitude to my awesome beta-readers, Caroline Lee and Jolene Stewart, for their suggestions and advice. And double thanks to Julie Tague, for being a truly excellent editor and assistant!

Click here for a complete list of other works by Merry Farmer.